AFRICA'S RELEASE

THE JOURNEY CONTINUES

BY MARK WENTLING

A PEACE CORPS WRITERS BOOK

AFRICA'S RELEASE
A Peace Corps Writers Book
An Imprint of Peace Corps Worldwide

Printed in the United States of America
by Peace Corps Writers of Oakland, California

For more information, contact peacecorpsworldwide@gmail.com. Peace Corps Writers and the Peace Corps Writers colophon are trademarks of PeaceCorpsWorldwide.org

ISBN: 193592544X
ISBN-13: 9781935925446

Library of Congress Control Number: 2014937004

First Peace Corps Writers Edition, April 2014

"…The novel succeeds as a portrait of a fascinating village and its politics.... The villagers' communal struggles and triumphs, especially when facing off against governmental officials, make for a compelling story. It's somewhat surprising to find a white foreigner ... so enthusiastically embraced as a spiritual talisman among the villagers; regardless, throughout the novel, the culture's traditions are visible, such as the detailed ritual that makes [the white man's] son their new chief. There's plenty of momentum as readers come to discover how various story lines intertwine..."

Kirkus Review

Dedicated to the Blessed Abyssinian

CONTENTS

AUTHOR'S NOTE

My first book, "Africa's Embrace," left too many unanswered questions. This sequel answers most of those questions, but not all. I now see that the telling of this African saga will not be complete without one more book. It will therefore require a "trilogy" to finish this lengthy story and allow me to share with you more fully what much of my lifetime in Africa has been like.

If you enjoyed reading my first book, you will appreciate this second book. If you did not read my first book, I believe you will find this second book a worthy read. My hope is that the reading of this second book will prompt you to read the first book. It is only by reading both books, and the one to follow, that you can fully master this complicated course on Africa and what it means for an American from Kansas to live and work there for over four decades..

While the focus is on Africa and the challenges posed to human progress on the diverse continent, the connection of the central character to Kansas is an important feature of both books. I seek to take the reader on an adventurous journey into the heart of Africa to confront many difficult issues and unanticipated events. I continue with my desire to educate, entertain, and enlighten the reader. I will have been a success if the reader finishes this trilogy with a good appreciation of what it means to be born in one place and made in another, as well as knowing how incredibly difficult it is to achieve lasting developmental advances in Africa.

I thank again all the people acknowledged in my previous book. I would like to add a few names to my previous list of former Peace Corps Volunteers I have known, and who have made Africa a big part of their lives. These additional names include: Peter Persell, Douglas Steinberg, Kelly Bishop, and Steven Amodio. I know that there are others— those I know and don't know—who I am over-looking, and thus, I will probably have more names to add in my last book in this African trilogy. In any event, I salute all those American Peace Corps Volunteers who remained behind after completing their service to make Africa their home.

I continue to be deeply indebted to Richard Feutz who has closely accompanied me during every step of the writing process from his home base in Mount Horeb, Wisconsin. His unfailing, enthusiastic reviews of multiple versions of each chapter were cru-cial to my book writing process. At this late stage in my life, he has made me see more clearly the many benefits of a genuine friend-ship that started in the Peace Corps in 1967.

This sequel is a work of fiction, but it is inspired by the actual experiences I have had in every corner of Africa since I first arrived in West Africa in 1970. Of course, having been born and raised in Kansas provides me with ample background for those chapters based in that part of the world. Obviously, I am responsible for every word written and all places and people referred to in my book are fictitious. This book...like my previous book and the one to come…has been writing itself in my head for nearly forty years, waiting to spill onto these pages.

My main wish is that all Africans who have the opportunity to read my books find them to their liking. I also wish that all non-Africans who know Africa well will be delighted to read what I have written. I will have fully achieved my mission if those who have not had any connection with Africa find my books instructive and a joy to read.

Mark Wentling
Ouagadougou, Burkina Faso
May 2014

CHAPTER ONE
J.B.

J.B. Jelly Button was taking his morning walk. Every day at sunrise he would walk in a very determined manner along the same path without paying the slightest attention to his surroundings. He would set off each morning dressed only in his red boxer shorts and white jersey undershirt, no matter the weather or the season. The timing of his morning walks was so regular that people could set their watches as he passed them by. Many would rise early to peer out their windows to watch him. People felt inspired by his glowing countenance and the purposeful manner he unfailingly took his daily walk. Referring to the regularity of his walks had become a popular figure of speech. When people wanted to affirm the veracity of what they were saying, they would insist, "It is as certain as J.B.'s morning walks."

J.B.'s walk took him straight along the road that ran in front of the small, ramshackle house he lived in with his older brother and his wife. He would walk across his neighbors' yards to the end of the block and make several zigzag patterns before cutting in a circular fashion through more yards to join a backstreet that was bordered by a small stream. He would crouch down at the same place along the stream and scoop up water with both hands, throwing it into the air five times as he mumbled some strange words. In winter, if there were ice on the water, he would break it with his fist. If he could not break the ice, he would still act as if he were throwing water into the air five times.

Oddly, the curious example set by J.B. encouraged people to adopt positive attitudes and to change their behaviors in a way that made them more successful in pursuing their lives' objectives. J.B.'s example helped them to work harder, be more persistent and disciplined. J.B.'s behavior encouraged them to never give up and focus on what they wanted to achieve. The way J.B. behaved was encapsulated in many phrases people would use to inspire themselves on to bigger and better things. For instance, people would often say, "Break the ice," to mean keep going no matter what and, "Even if you cannot break the ice, you should not give up." Through J.B.'s daily, zany example, people learned to be more thankful for what they had and not to let the troubles of life depress them. Having J.B. around was like having an extra boost in life; he was quickly becoming a bizarre but highly admired cult figure.

After his brief stop at the stream, J.B. would walk back through the neighborhood and go straight to his house. He had taken that walk so many times over the years, there was a well-worn path referred to as "J.B.'s" path. People had measured the length of the path to be about eight hundred yards. Some people speculated the outline of the path represented something. A sketch of the path's outline had been drawn, and it became part of a popular red T-shirt imprint. Many wore the T-shirt that displayed a sketch of the outline of the path with the letters, "J.B.'s Path," boldly printed in black in the center of the outline. The shirt design was copyrighted by J.B.'s neighbors. The copyright was sold to a large manufacturer of T-shirts and a percentage of all sales were deposited in the "Save J.B. Fund" account that had been opened in a local bank.

Initially, people complained about J.B.'s antics and his trespassing, but when they confronted him they were calmed and at a loss for words when they looked into his angelic face. J.B. had a mesmerizing gaze that made people not want to interfere with the mission, whatever it was, of that harmless individual. One look into J.B.'s greenish, but piercing eyes, was usually enough to put even the most cantankerous person into an agreeable mood. It was as if those who peered deeply into his eyes were placed under a magical spell. After many years, nobody would bother J.B., and he was never a bother to anyone. He became something of a treasured neighborhood oddity who enjoyed celebrity status. J.B.'s path became a protected area that everyone knew not to disturb.

J.B. had a large potbelly and a huge belly button. His belly would shake like jelly with his every step. Years ago some neighborhood kids taunted him as he passed by, calling him J.B. Jelly Button. The name stuck. Eventually, people simply referred to him as J.B. In fact, nobody knew his real name or anything about why he behaved as he did. Some of the older people in the neighborhood in the small town of Gemini, Kansas said they had heard rumors that J.B. had spent some time in Africa and returned home in an altered state of mind. They had heard second hand that he had suffered from a severe case of something called cultural shock and had never recovered from the trauma caused by his experiences in Africa.

J.B.'s skin always looked like it had been burnt red by prolonged exposure to the elements. He was bald and had a pug nose. His spindly arms and legs dangled awkwardly from a short body of asymmetrical proportions. Particularly noticeable were his calloused and scabby knees. People thought his knees were like that because he often kneeled on the ground to tend the goldfish he raised in a pool in his tiny backyard. It was rumored that he spoke to his goldfish in a strange language. On rare occasions people had heard him talking to himself in an unintelligible language as he took his morning walks. His voice sounded like a scratchy old record turned on low volume at the wrong speed. His words seemed to struggle to move from his vocal cords to his mouth. As he seldom spoke, most of what people said about what he muttered was more rumor than fact.

J.B.'s hands were well calloused and his fingernails were cracked and often filthy. He was constantly working the soil of his small vegetable garden and tending the wide variety of plants he kept around his house in old tin cans and plastic bags. He had plants of every kind, including some plants that nobody had seen before. He kept many plants inside. His small bedroom was covered with plants, top to bottom, barely leaving any room for his narrow little bed. Tending his plants and goldfish always kept him busy, but none of his other tasks would prevent him from taking his daily morning walk. When he needed money, he would put up a small white flag in his front yard to indicate he had goldfish for sale. Nobody knew what he did with his money, but it was suspected he gave it to his older brother.

J.B. also kept in his room a collection of various reptiles, keeping each one in a small cage that he had built himself. He also kept in cages a large variety of birds. Cats were attracted to him and a large number of them had taken up residence at his place. His room smelled so badly that his brother blocked it off from the rest of the house and built for J.B. his own outside door. J.B.'s elderly brother and his wife were recluses and never spoke to anyone.

Their origins were something of a mystery. It was believed their house was the first house in the neighborhood, having been a farm that had become part of the town over forty years ago. They were rarely seen outside and nobody had ever seen them together with J.B. They were the only ones who could possibly know what had happened to J.B., but they did not talk to anyone. They seemed intent on taking J.B.'s secret, if indeed they knew his secret, to the grave with them. People thought all they were doing was waiting to die.

One thing that intrigued the neighborhood most about J.B. was the exceptional run he would take along his footpath every time the moon was at its fullest. He seemed to be energized by the full moon and ran at an unbelievably fast pace. His features seemed to alter under the light of the full moon and he became much stronger. He also talked more during the full moon phase, mostly to his fish, reptiles, cats, birds, and plants. It was obvious that his captivating madness peaked when he was exposed to the rays of the full moon. Some nights he could be seen standing for a very long time in his backyard with his arms outstretched, staring at the full moon. He seemed to be waiting for something that only he could know about.

The neighborhood and local community adored J.B. His story traveled far and wide, and people would drive long distances to see him go on his morning walk. The neighborhood protected him from any undesirable incursions into his privacy, but it could not hide his growing notoriety. Reports of him had appeared in the newspapers and on TV. All the attention went unnoticed by J.B. He went about his usual routines as if there was nobody around. It did not matter to him what other people said or did. The only things that really mattered to him were his daily routines and the call of the full moon.

All the publicity caught the attention of local health authorities, who said his house was a source of potential disease and should be condemned. They also said J.B. should be admitted to the institution for the mentally ill on "third hill" in a neighboring town. (There were three hills in the town. On top of one was a prison, on another was an orphanage, and on the last hill was a mental institution. An often-heard threat was to be told you were going to be sent to one hill or another, depending on the applicable case.) When J.B.'s neighbors heard about the threat against their beloved J.B., they filed a protest and organized a well-publicized demonstration in favor of keeping J.B. where he lived and in the same conditions. They assured everyone they would take care of "their" J.B. Local authorities acceded to the popular pressure and ceased all efforts to remove him. Upon hearing the news that the authorities would allow J.B. to stay put, a neighborhood block party was held and donations were collected for the "Save J.B. Fund."

It was a mystery as to what J.B. ate. As he had a big belly and was always in good health, he must have been eating well, but people were uncertain about what he consumed. Some believed he ate his goldfish. His brother and sister were never seen buying groceries, and J.B. never ventured beyond the area outlined by his path. What did they eat? That question was often on the minds of his neighbors and they worried he did not have enough to eat. Neighbors would often send their children with food baskets and leftovers to leave in front of J.B.'s door. Those offerings always disappeared, and the baskets were left empty. Therefore, people were convinced he was consuming their generous gifts. There were some dark rumors that he ate the animals and plants he raised, and fed most of the food given to him by the neighbors to his animals.

J.B.'s body almost always looked very clean. Some people had seen him late at night washing his body from a bucket of water he had fetched from the small artificial pond he had built for his goldfish. He scrubbed his body from top to bottom, but he never removed his red boxer shorts, and it was not known if he had more than one pair of shorts. People would sometimes leave an extra pair of the same kind of shorts in the food baskets they delivered to his house. He stood on a large stone while he bathed and sometimes he could be observed sitting on that same stone while he fanned the flames in a small wire brazier. He would build a small fire in that brazier and cook something that he would chomp on firmly with his big white teeth, swallowing whatever it was with much gusto and animalistic grunts of satisfaction. He was often chewing on a small stick, which he also used to rub his teeth and gums. In all things, weird as they seemed, J.B. acted exactly as if he knew what he was doing.

There were other rumors about J.B. Some thought that maybe he had been taken away by aliens and returned home, and now he was waiting for his alien friends to return for him. Others thought he had been a war veteran who had been brainwashed by the enemy. Another rumor was that J.B. was a walking corpse trying to leave the world to join the dead. People had waited for years to see what J.B.'s ultimate fate would be.

Children who grew up in the neighborhood were often scolded for their misbehavior with the words, "Why can't you behave like the sweet, dear old J.B. who does not bother anyone?" Children were taught to love and respect J.B. When children became adults and left the area to strike out on their own, they missed J.B. They would write home to ask for the latest news about J.B. When asked to write stories or poems at school, children would write about J.B. For many, J.B. was an uncanny central part of their lives.

The whole town was prepared to give J.B. a very big funeral when he died. J.B.'s intriguing existence had made their lives so much more interesting and had broken up the monotony of small-town life. As strange and eccentric as J.B. was, everyone was thankful for his presence among them. Somehow he conferred upon them a much appreciated spiritual uplifting. Some believed he was an angel in disguise sent by God. They could not imagine life without J.B.'s odd behavior to observe and talk about. Many prayed for J.B. to remain among them for a very long time. As strange as it sounds, the incomprehensible, idiotic J.B. had become larger than life and a local legend. It was indeed a majestic case of madness at its best.

CHAPTER TWO
BOBOVOVI

J.B. had been to Africa. The truth was that a couple of decades ago he had spent years working to help the poor in the Ataku District in the impoverished West African country of Kotonu. Something had happened to him there, and he was evacuated back to his home in Kansas. It was not clear how things ended for him in Africa, but it was obvious that he had become deranged and authorities were obliged to send him home. An investigation was made into his case by the US Embassy, but its conclusions were ambiguous. The final evacuation order for J.B. just said he was suffering from severe trauma caused by extreme cross-cultural immersion.

For the people of the village of Ataku it was very clear what had happened. J.B. had spent several years in the village of Ataku and became very involved with the people and their customs. As J.B. was born on a Tuesday, they renamed him in their local language "Bobovovi," which literarily meant "Tuesday's white child." His name was often abbreviated to simply "Bobo." The village adopted Bobo and considered him a special person, particularly as it was evident to them that their grandfathers (ancestors) and the traditional gods and spirits they worshiped were attracted to Bobo and trying to communicate through him. It was as if their "other world" had been waiting for a long time for Bobo to arrive. The village's leaders worked to fulfill his destiny and to determine how it would affect their village.

Bobo experienced many strange and wonderful things. He rode a moonbeam, was attacked by the local ogre, Ajaja, and his house was invaded by army ants. But the most amazing thing that happened was an off-season rain that fell only on his house and resulted in the mysterious sprouting of baobab tree seedlings around his house. The unprecedented sign was interpreted by the village chief, Yofu, and his most senior advisors and fetish priests as an invitation for Bobo from the most ancient baobab tree in the district. Bobo was taken to the tree by five men selected by the chief and ended up staying all night within the hollow of the tree.

The five men who accompanied Bobo waited all night for him to exit the tree. They were hoping the old baobab would communicate some secrets to Bobo that had been lost to the village for generations. In particular, they wanted to relearn the secret of the five leaves. In their village history, there were repeated references to that important secret, which had five elements, one for each of the five leaves that composed an entire baobab leaf cluster. The people of the village believed regaining knowledge of that secret would greatly enhance their stature and power.

Bobo exited the tree at dawn the following morning. He had learned all the secrets the five men wanted to know, but when he tried to speak to them about it, they did not hear him. At first, Bobo could not understand why the men did not notice him. He eventually realized he was invisible to them and had been transformed into a spirit form during his long night inside the ancient baobab tree. In that form he felt as if he were human, but he was like a ghost. He could see everyone and roam the village as he pleased, but nobody could see or hear him. Life went on in the village, but Bobo, in his new spirit form, remained the same.

The news of Bobo's disappearance while inside the old baobab shook the village like a major earthquake. Its seismic reverberations spread more quickly than the speed of sound. When people heard the astounding news about Bobo, they stopped what they were doing and became almost paralyzed by the profound dramatic nature of the news of the unprecedented event. It was as if a sonic shock wave of unimaginable proportions had hit the village and left everyone in a state of trauma. The magnitude of what happened to Bobo was beyond their comprehension and people were unable to cope. Some people collapsed on the spot.

The days passed and people remained idle as they attempted to recover from the immensity of Bobo's miraculous disappearance and probable transformation into a spirit. They waited helplessly for their leaders to explain what had happened and to tell them what to do. People stopped eating, drinking, and sleeping, and lay weak like lumps of flesh wrapped in unwashed rags. The chief and his elders felt the same, but they knew immediate action was needed to prevent the entire village from perishing. The chief was in a much enfeebled state, but he mustered enough energy to call a village assembly and consult with his elders and senior fetish priests about what he should say to the villagers.

The chief sat silently for several hours with his senior advisors. Nobody knew what to say and their minds were overwhelmed by what had happened to Bobo. Their bodies were so weak it was hard to find the energy to say anything. Finally, the eldest among them managed to say softly, "We must do something, as it is highly likely that Bobo's spirit is among us and we need to honor him."

Another elder weakly exclaimed, "Yes, we need to make him know we appreciate his sacrifice. We need to find a way to communicate with him."

Chief Yofu and other elders started to fidget, trying to formulate words in their mouths so they could also join into the discussion. Eventually, they all agreed that their main mission was to show high recognition to Bobo for his stunning transformation. They strongly believed they could best do that by profoundly changing their own lives to conform to what they knew would be pleasing to Bobo. They had no doubt that Bobo was now in the other world with the grandfathers and the diverse pantheon of traditional gods and spirits. Indeed, Bobo must have had an exalted place in that pantheon and, therefore, deserved to be worshiped like a prominent divinity.

The main conclusion of the village council meeting was that everyone should be instructed to behave as Bobo would have liked to have seen when he lived among them. Everyone would be asked to reflect deeply and see how they could change their nature to better fit the vision of the new and improved future that Bobo had always wished for the village. The people would be told to work harder, discipline themselves, and be prepared to sacrifice in order to please Bobo. Everyone would be called upon to transcend their very beings so Bobo could justify to all those in the other world why their village deserved to be so blessed.

The next day at the appointed hour, people gathered in the large opening near the old kapok tree to listen to what Chief Yofu would say. In an unusual gesture of solidarity, Chief Gyasi of the neighboring village of Aniko and many of his subjects joined the huge assembly. It was the first time anyone could remember the ferociously opposing village participating in an assembly meeting called by Chief Yofu. The presence of Chief Gyasi and so many people from

Aniko prompted people to think that maybe the long feud between the two villages could be resolved. Chief Yofu walked slowly and, exceptionally, alone to a point in the center of all those assembled. In another unusual gesture, he was not wearing his chief's hat, and he walked without his traditional cane. He also wore the simplest of gowns. His intention was to convey humbleness and the absence of pride.

Chief Yofu raised both hands in front of him to indicate he was ready to speak. The already very hushed crowd became even quieter. The chief took a long time to utter his first words. It was as if he were struggling to release the words he had to say. Looking up into the sky, he finally said softly in a sad, melancholy tone, "Bobo."

The chief repeated Bobo's name many times, and each time he said that saintly name he said it louder and with more force. It was as if he was calling Bobo, as well as preparing to talk to the crowd. The absence of his hat, cane, and usual entourage indicated that he was presenting himself as a simple man from the earthly world with a contrite heart. It was apparent that he was ready to submit to Bobo and those he was with in the other world. The people were in tears and trembling because of the very sincere and humble way the chief was surrendering himself, and by doing so, offering up his entire village to the will of Bobo.

Chief Yofu continued beseeching the heaatibonvens with the following solemn words, "Bobo, we regret your passing, but we know you have gone to a special place in the other world. We want you to know we appreciate and admire you for having done what no man has ever done before. From now on, we want to do all we can, in our minds and deeds, in a way that is pleasing to you. We want your grace to always shine on us, and we will always pray for your blessing. You are with us now more than ever before. We promise to change our ways and live the vision we know you desired for us. You will always be in the center of our thoughts and we will show you unfailing homage at your new home in the ancient baobab tree. We ask that you look over us and help us as we endeavor to become newly reborn as you would like."

The chief said his words slowly and distinctly in order to allow everyone to set them firmly in their minds. He paused a long time between his phrases so his words would sink deeply into the minds of the people. He concluded by looking directly into the crowd and saying, "You have heard my words. I now ask that all of you to begin working to make it so. In the following days I will be issuing additional instructions on actions we will undertake in the name of Bobo. From that day on, it will be a new day in our village, and we will all work to create a better way forward in honor of Bobo."

Just as the crowd was ready to break up, the Chief of Aniko, Gyasi, humbly asked to speak. He also came forward in a simple traditional gown, bare headed, and not in his usual businesslike safari suit. He stood next to Chief Yofu. The crowd collectively swallowed hard when he made the unprecedented gesture of close friendship by clutching Chief Yofu's hand. While holding Chief Yofu's hand, Chief Gyasi looked into the sky for a long moment, and then briefly addressed all those present by saying, "We now have the obligation to honor in our daily lives the past human presence of Bobo by showing his spirit, which is now always present among us, our goodwill and sincerity in doing as he would like us to do."

In a serious and deep voice, he concluded by proclaiming, "Bobo will always be with us and we must do all we can to demonstrate to him we are trying our best to improve our lives as he asked us to do while he was among us in his previous earthly life. We have no choice but to work to please Bobo. Doing anything else would result in severe consequences for our villages and all the people of the District of Ataku."

When Chief Gyasi finished speaking, he hesitated awkwardly for a few minutes, and then he turned to embrace Chief Yofu. That powerful gesture between the leaders of two villages that had been feuding for generations caused great rejoicing among the crowd. Many people were in tears and everybody was hugging all those around them. Loud shouts of "amen," and "hallelujah" were heard as people began singing together vibrant songs of praise to Bobo. It was as if at that moment their world began to transform itself.

The longer that joyous event lasted, the deeper it was felt by the people. The chiefs stood in amazement with teary eyes as people openly wept and fell to the ground, prostrate with joy and wonderment over the transcending nature of what was happening. It was many hours before the last group of people could find sufficient strength and clarity to return to their homes. All night long people sat silently thinking of how the next day they would work with the community to begin the challenging but exalting task of honoring Bobo. People were deeply afraid they would not be able to respond sufficiently to Bobo's wishes. Yet, they knew that with the dawning of the next day, they must do something to demonstrate to Bobo the sincerity of their hearts and their high respect for him.

CHAPTER THREE
CELESTINE

While everyone was preoccupied with how they could change their behavior and deeply ingrained habits in a way that would be pleasing to Bobo, there was a young woman in Aniko who was focused on other matters. That troubled woman was Celestine, who, a few weeks earlier, had an amorous couple of hours with Bobo on a rainy day. They had made love, or what was referred to as "war" in the local culture, and Celestine was pregnant with an unwanted child. Her predicament was complicated because Bobo was no longer an earthly being whom she could inform of her condition. Moreover, nobody would believe that Bobo was the man responsible for her pregnancy. She had nowhere to go and nobody to tell her story. Without Bobo around, she was in a real fix.

Abortion was out of the question, especially since Bobo had crossed into the spirit world and he was believed to have been elevated to a high level among the hundreds of divinities in that other world. She felt duty bound to have the child and provide the care a child of a new divinity deserved. Yet, she was desperate for some sign from Bobo that would communicate to everyone his acceptance of the child growing in her belly. Better yet, she wanted Bobo to return to Earth to be her husband and a caring father for their child. All her thoughts were about how to get Bobo back and not about how to please Bobo. She knew of only one person who might be able to help her. That person was Atiwono, the aged woman who had mastered all there was to know about the value of plants and almost anything else about nature.

Celestine patiently waited for a day when she could discreetly sneak away without being seen. That day finally came. She took back paths to Atiwono's secluded compound in the deep woods where the mountain slope began to climb steeply. She arrived at Atiwono's disorderly compound to find her in a woeful state. Atiwono was lying on a grass mat like an ancient pile of disorganized, loosely packed baggage. She looked more pitiful than usual, and she was barely breathing. The young man who worked as her caretaker tried to alert her to the arrival of Celestine by making a loud, hissing noise. He made the noise repeatedly, but Atiwono did not stir from her position. Her tiny eyes remained closed and buried deep within her shrunken face.

Celestine cautiously approached Atiwono and knelt down beside her. She took her swollen little hand in hers and began to sing softly a song she knew would be pleasing to the ears of Atiwono. She repeated her enchanting tune several times, but Atiwono remained as if in a coma. She kept singing as she squeezed more tightly Atiwono's hand. After some time, Atiwono's eyes opened and she looked at Celestine and forced her puckered little mouth into a crooked semblance of a smile. Their eyes locked briefly. At that moment, Celestine believed there was hope of recovering her beloved Bobo.

Words began to bubble and burp from Atiwono's fishlike mouth. Her caretaker lifted her from the ground and placed her gently in a nearby armchair. She sat still for a few moments, and then beckoned for Celestine to come closer so they could communicate. Atiwono struggled to utter some words Celestine could understand. She spoke in slobbery fits and spurts. She started by sputtering, "My dear, I am so happy you have come. I have been waiting for you. You came almost too late, as I am in my last days on this Earth. My time has come after more than a hundred years to join those in the other world."

Celestine found it hard to control her emotions at hearing such words from Atiwono. Tears began to run down her high cheekbones. Her grief over Atiwono's lamentable condition made it difficult for her to focus on what she needed to say to Atiwono. She wiped her tears, cleared her throat, and spoke softly into Atiwono's right ear. "Mama Atiwono, I am sorry to bother you, but I need your help. You know what happened to Bobo. I need Bobo back, as I am carrying his child. I have nowhere to go and all is lost for me if Bobo cannot come back and recognize his child." After saying those words, Celestine choked up and could not continue. Before she could say more, Atiwono intervened.

"Dear child, you do not have to talk. I know why you are here. I will do everything I can with my remaining powers to bring Bobo back to you and the people of Ataku. I have a plan, but for that plan to work you must agree to one important thing."

Celestine's spirits brightened and she quickly asked, "What 'thing' is that?"

Atiwono hesitated a moment, as if trying to catch her breath, and then whispered in her raspy voice, "You must agree to take my place."

Celestine became faint and took a step back when she heard that command dribbling out of the mouth of Atiwono. That was the last thing she expected to hear. She was shocked. Her first impulse was to turn around and leave. For her, it was preposterous to think that she could ever replace Mama Atiwono. After some moments, in a trembling voice Celestine said, "Please, Mama Atiwono, you cannot be serious. Of all people, you should know that I am not the one to replace you."

Atiwono took some time to say tenderly in a hushed voice, "My dear child, I cannot help myself. You have been chosen by all the plants I have been living with all my life. There is no other way but to accept and obey. You need to know the only way you can get Bobo back is to replace me and work with the plants and trees. There must be a way for the ancient baobab to return Bobo to us. Only the plants can know how do to this."

Celestine was at a loss for words. She had never imagined that her destiny would place her in Atiwono's messy, odoriferous garden. She had always fancied herself as a well-to-do chief's daughter who would be married to a wealthy man and taken away to live in the city. It was impossible for her to accept that her destiny lay there in the bush, in a dumpy shack, and the stink of rotting vegetation with hundreds of birds and dozens of cats. Her mind could not cope. She collapsed and fell to the ground, lying in a comatose state. As Celestine lay motionless, Atiwono and her caretaker calmly stood by. They waited for her to regain consciousness.

Atiwono asked her caretaker to bring some leaves from a small bush growing at the perimeter of her jungle-like compound. She took two handfuls of those leaves and cupped them in her hands, blowing softly on them while she muttered some unintelligible words. She crushed the leaves by rubbing them between her hands and blew the particles so they landed on top of Celestine's prostrate body. When the last particle of those leafy fragments fell on Celestine, she began to wake up.

Celestine slowly came to her senses and sat straight-up with her legs flat on the ground in front of her. She looked around at her shabby surroundings, seeing plants growing everywhere and vines dangling from old trees. Birds of all sorts were flying excitedly overhead, and cats were meowing strangely in a loud chorus. She kept asking herself how that could possibly become the place where she would spend the rest of her life. She abruptly wailed loudly in a high-pitched voice, asking the gods in rapid-fire fashion why they had given her such a destiny. The very thought of replacing Atiwono revolted her to the core. Over and over she hysterically screamed, "Why me?"

Atiwono was experiencing a mixture of joy and pity over Celestine's plight, but her joy over having a person to whom she could finally pass on her knowledge of the plant kingdom was so high, she felt rejuvenated. While Celestine sat agonizing over her fateful predicament, Atiwono was already thinking about how she could train Celestine in the shortest possible time. She was also considering ways she could help Celestine bring Bobo back. She looked at Celestine and sympathetically said, "I know, my child, this is very hard to accept, but you are the one chosen to replace me. You must accept your destiny with courage and commit yourself fully to it. Surrender to the will of the plants and the spirits of the other world, and find harmony and purpose in your life. If there is any hope of you ever seeing Bobo again, you must happily accept your destiny and make a great success of it."

Celestine listened carefully to Atiwono's words. She remained quiet and inanimate for a long time after Atiwono had spoken those words. She took her time to stand up and brush herself off. She stood as erect as she could and looked deeply into Atiwono's filmy, yellow-brown eyes and simply said, "When and how can I start?"

Atiwono responded like a bird chirping with delight, "Tomorrow. Come early in the morning with enough of your things to stay here with me. Your initial training will be intense and last for over a month. If your father needs to know more, tell him to come and see me. Please do not worry. You will be all right and everything will go better than you expect."

Celestine abruptly turned around and, without another word, started walking home at a slow pace. Sometimes she had trouble making her feet move. She paused and sat down several times at the side of the path. She took many deep breaths; she was in a state of shock. She was angry that her ultimate, but unwanted, fate had revealed itself in such an abrupt and unexpected manner. It was taking time for all that had happened at Atiwono's to sink into her mind. She still could not fully digest the implications of the sudden change in her life's course. It was difficult for her to accept that her days as a pretty, fancy chief's daughter were over. She was now obliged to live like a dirty gardener in a soiled patch of forest, learning all about the medicinal and magical powers of plants. It was beyond her how she could survive such a profound transformation in her circumstances and life plan. The only thing keeping her going was the thought that she must do her best so that she could find a way to bring Bobo back. She was ready to sacrifice herself and do all Mama Atiwono asked her to do. She felt growing within her a strong commitment to be the best at what Mama Atiwono did so she could gain the powers and knowledge needed to bring Bobo back.

When Celestine returned home, she quickly greeted her father and mother, rapidly telling them in a matter-of-fact, calm manner that she was moving out in the morning to go live with Atiwono.

Her parents' surprise at hearing that alarming news was deeply disconcerting. They sat quietly, not saying a word, as they did not know what to do. They both knew if what Celestine said was true, there was nothing they could do to change the radical new course in her life. They knew their lovely daughter would never say such a thing if it had not come from higher powers. Obviously, she had come from seeing Atiwono, and that meant whatever transpired between her and the powerful old woman was beyond their meager capacities to change. They could only help their daughter to pack and accompany her to Atiwono's place the next morning. The mold of Celestine's destiny had been cast long ago. There was nothing to be done now except surrender and heed the obligatory call of her destiny as it had been fully revealed.

CHAPTER FOUR
ROADWORK

elestine was not the only one to lay sleepless that night. Almost everyone in the villages of Ataku and Aniko experienced a restless night as they contemplated the unprecedented work they would do together the next day. After deep reflection and extensive consultation, the chiefs of the two villages decided the best way to start honoring Bobo was to do one of the tasks he was overheard saying should be done. Bobo believed strongly that the villages should band together and maintain the roads leading to and from the villages, particularly the road connecting the villages to the main national highway.

Years ago it had been part of the villages' community work routine to maintain the roads and cut back the encroachment of brush on the sides of the roads. Villagers would also line the roads with large stones and paint them with whitewash. Following independence, government officials informed the villages they no longer needed to maintain the roads in their areas, as that, henceforth, would be the government's responsibility. Shortly after conveying that information, the government sent a road grader and many workers to put the roads in good condition. That first instance of government road improvements ended up being the last time the government did anything to maintain the roads. After the passing of many years, there was no longer any hope that the government would help maintain the roads.

Over the years, the roads had deteriorated greatly and brush had encroached on them, narrowing the roadbed in many places to only a footpath. Bobo was heard saying several times, "You know that the government will not be doing anything more for the roads. Therefore, you need to do as you did in the old days and take care of the roads yourselves. If you do not act soon, your roads will disappear and even four-wheeled vehicles will no longer be able to access your villages. How can there be any progress without good roads?"

After much deliberation, the chiefs had decided their first gesture in honor of Bobo would be to reintroduce road maintenance days. All able-bodied adults would be expected to work and bring any tools they had that could be used to return the roads to their original condition. Each family and clan would be assigned a stretch of road that would be their responsibility to return it to its original condition and ensure its future maintenance. Everyone was expected to volunteer and rise early every Monday and Thursday to work on the roads until they were in their original condition. After that had been achieved, every Thursday would be dedicated to road maintenance.

The chiefs announced jointly that fines and punishment would be imposed on any slackers who did not do their part to fix the roads. Laziness was declared a source of the villages' development problems and, therefore, would no longer be tolerated. Everyone would have to work, the educated as well as the uneducated. Only the old and sick would be exempt from the work obligation.

The chiefs called on their subjects to demonstrate goodwill and a changed behavior that would please Bobo. They had to show Bobo they could work well together in full harmony and with common purpose. The chiefs said they had a new vision for their villages. From that point on, their two villages would strive to become models for the rest of the region to follow. They repeatedly noted it was only the start of more improvements to come.

As the sun rose over Mount Ataku, hundreds of villagers were positioning themselves at their assigned places along the sides of all the roads leading in and out of the villages. They were dressed in their work clothes and carried with them a variety of hand-tools, shovels, picks, machetes, and hoes. The women had with them baskets and metallic basins, which could be used to carry earth and gravel on their heads. Children were on standby to collect any debris and useable wood that could be recuperated from cutting the brush back to within five yards of the sides of the roads. Some men also had axes with them. It would be necessary to chop down trees growing too close to the roads and to cut tree branches, which cast too much shade on the road, thus contributing to the softening of the earthen roadbed.

People stood quietly with their heads down as they waited for the chiefs to instruct the gong-gong men to kick off the workday by banging on their bifurcated hollow iron horns. The chiefs' guards trotted up and down the roadsides to make sure everyone was in place and ready to start work. One guard signaled to the other with a short toot from a wooden whistle when his section of the road was ready to begin work. After some time, the guard nearest the chiefs gave the final toot on his whistle. Upon hearing that melodic signal, the chiefs clasped hands and lifted their arms together. That was the sign the gong-gong men were waiting for, and they began madly beating their metal horns with hard steel rods, making a loud clanking noise. As they beat their cast iron instruments, they ran up and down the roads so all could know that now was the time to begin working.

The two chiefs stood still, holding hands as they watched unfold before them a new way forward in the histories of their villages. They could not have imagined a few weeks ago that what was happening before their eyes was possible. They were both praising Bobo in soft voices and thanking him for opening new doors by his miraculous passage to the other world. Nobody would have believed that such opposing chiefs with different backgrounds could come together in the name of achieving progress in the name of Bobo. It was indeed a newly created world unfolding before them.

They made for an odd-looking pair. Chief Yofu of Ataku was old, short, and very corpulent, and always dressed in traditional clothes. Chief Gyasi of Aniko was younger, tall and thin, and always dressed in a businesslike safari suit. Yofu wore flat, locally made goat leather sandals. Gyasi wore shiny imported black dress shoes and nylon socks. Yofu's skin had a brownish tone, while Gyasi's was very dark. Yofu had many wives; Gyasi was monogamous. Yet, they were cousins who had passed all their lives without talking to each other because of an ancient feud between their villages.

Both chiefs were very happy to be reunited and working closely together. They were in total agreement that Bobo had opened a new path of enlightenment that they had to follow together. They knew that meant forgetting and forgiving all previous clashes between their two villages. They had developed together a shared vision for a better future for the people, especially for the younger generation. They were bound and determined that their grandchildren would inherit a better world than the one they knew.

The people threw themselves into the roadwork. Men were eager to begin cutting back the tall grasses and bushes that had overgrown the roadbed, but waited for one of the groups of drummers to come and make noise along their section of the road before putting their machetes and axes into play. The noise was to scare away the snakes and any evil spirits, which might be lurking in the brush. As soon as the last drummer pounded his last beat, energetic chopping started. So many blades were at work at once that it sounded like a gigantic lawn mower cutting down the woods.

As the men chopped madly away, the women gathered with their hands the loose grass, leaves, and twigs, and piled them in the middle of the roadbed. Other women would come and remove from those piles any wooden sticks that could be used for firewood. They would make small stacks of that wood, and then children would come and tie the stacks into bundles with straps cut from tree vines. They would head-carry those bundles back to newly designated common firewood storage places in the villages. Once all useable wood was removed, old women would come with hot coals from their cooking fires and set alight the remaining piles in the road. The burning of the debris in that manner not only disposed of it, but the heat from the fire helped harden the clay in the roadbed.

All along the road, elderly women had set up small outdoor cooking stands to make food for the workers. Groups of children were busy delivering food and water to all those in need. Mounds of white corn mush and okra sauce were provided to all those who were hungry and calabash bowls of cool, clear water were given to those who were thirsty. Huge clay pots of palm wine were kept on hand for celebrating the end of the day's work. The visibility of the clay pots was a great incentive for the men to work as hard as they could.

As the men peeled back the brush from the sides of the road, the women would come with their short-handled hoes and scrape the ground clean of any remaining weeds. Another group of men with shovels followed the women and dug a shallow trench at the edge of the roads for drainage purposes during the rainy season. The earth they dug out to make those trenches was thrown back onto the roadbed and spread about by another group of women armed with hoes to fill any potholes, making the road as level and smooth as possible. It was quite an inspiring sight to see all that activity going on at once. The hot and profusely perspiring group of people was sure that Bobo was smiling down upon them.

At a few spots along the road, there were huge trees that had to be cut down and moved away from the road. Moving those felled trees required the collective forces of many men from several groups. Responding to the call for help, men came running from other sections of the road to join with others to push a felled tree deep into the bush. At first when they pushed, they could barely budge the tree. They tried mightily to roll the tree trunk into the bush, but they could not make it move. Finally, as they were pushing as hard as they could against the trunk, one man cried out, "Please help us, Bobo!"

Then, another man came up with a chant: "One, two, three— push for Bobo."

Upon hearing that, the men redoubled their efforts, pushed with the last ounce of their collective strength against the trunk, and repeated together those same words. When they said in unison the name, "Bobo," they pushed with all their might and the trunk began to roll. They did that same drill over and over until the heavy tree trunk was far from the roadside. From that day on, anytime anyone was faced with moving a heavy load, they would say "Bobo" as they strained to lift or shove the load.

The roadsides were cleared, the drainage ditches dug, and the earth removed from those ditches spread where needed on the roadbed. Yet, there were still uneven places and some potholes in the road that needed to be filled. That had been foreseen and another group of women arrived with tied cloth bundles or basins of laterite earth to fill in those places. Those women came from a long distance where laterite was abundant. The women dropped the red laterite into the holes and men with shovels spread it. Once all the depressions and holes in the roadbed were filled, the same men would pound hard on those places with the backs of their shovel blades.

When one group would finish its section of the road, they would join together to walk in their bare feet up and down their section, stomping hard on those places where there was loose dirt that needed to be compacted. As they walked, they began spontane- ously singing a little song that, basically, was composed of repeat- ing Bobo's name in different tones and levels of loudness. There was first a loud "Bobo" followed by a string of soft "Bobos." The men sang the first loud Bobo in deep bass voices and the women followed by repeating Bobo several times in soft, but high-pitched voices. The rhythm of that song was something like the chugging sound of an old locomotive "choo-choo" train. The people slowly marched in time to that tune, slapping their feet to the ground in perfect unison of movement every time the final syllable of Bobo was sounded.

The people were exhausted, but they were also very happy and filled with exceeding joy. They were pleased to see how much they could achieve by working together. They had forged new bonds and were already thinking that if they could fix the road as they had on that day, they could do anything. They were eager to know what would be the next task the chiefs would direct them to do.

The chiefs were also happy about how well things had gone and gave the order for the palm wine to be served. The people drank, sang, and danced with the little remaining energy they had to celebrate what had been achieved that day. The outstanding way the people performed had the chiefs' minds abuzz with more ideas about how they could make improvements in the lives of all. Their observations of the intensive hard labor that fixing the roads required moved the chiefs to think about introducing innovations that could make such work easier and faster to do. For example, they were asking themselves why they could not build wheelbarrows and introduce donkey carts. Their minds magically opened to so many things they had not before considered.

There was so much to do and they had lost too much time. They would have to work doubly hard and very intelligently to catch up to where they should have been years ago. They should not have waited so long to make the road like it was thirty years ago. It was as if their new future would be regaining what they had lost in the past. They could see that part of the daunting challenge they faced was akin to running ahead as fast as they could just to keep from slipping backward.

CHAPTER FIVE
ONE ROAD NOT DONE

The impressive roadwork the people of Ataku and Aniko had achieved made them feel very good about themselves. The road improvements they had undertaken together were serving as a useful demonstration to all twenty villages in the Ataku District except for one. While the positive spin-off from their roadwork was encouraging other villages to replicate similar efforts, one village remained untouched by the reinvigorating aftermath of Bobo's mysterious passage to the other world.

The village was Muvosho. Its people had learned about Bobo's amazing transformation and how Ataku and Aniko were uplifted by working diligently to honor him. They were in a quandary and worried about their fate. They were guilty of having abused Bobo's goodwill and causing him much stress. They feared Bobo's entry into the other world would result in terrible punishment for their misdeeds. They knew serious consequences would befall them if they did not do something quickly to show their remorse over the way they misled Bobo. Somehow they had to find a way to make right the wrong they had done.

Since the disappearance of Bobo, Muvosho's chief, Osakwe, rarely left his compound. He was too ashamed of what he had done to Bobo to face his fellow villagers. He had intentionally swindled Bobo and acted only in his own selfish interests. His dictatorial manner had disgusted everyone in his village. He was now living in fear of the wrath Bobo could inflict upon him in concert with other spirits and the grandfathers for his serious transgression against Bobo's good intentions. Osakwe was also fearful of what his own people might do to him. He could not sleep or eat. He suffered in every way and was in a miserable condition. His conscience tormented him. He knew he would be held accountable for his wrongful acts. He was too scared and ashamed to face his people.

Osakwe had accepted and expressed high appreciation of Bobo's gift of a village grinding mill, but once the mill and all its accessories were delivered to the village, he made it so Bobo could not return to the village. He had a huge kapok tree cut down to block the road between Ataku and Muvosho at a place where briar patches made it impossible to find another way to Muvosho. Bobo suffered physical injuries when he tried to walk through the briar patch, and he was mentally depressed about not being able to follow up with his promising mill project in Muvosho. Bobo tried many times to go to Muvosho, but his way was always blocked by the tree lying across the road. He could not understand why the people of Muvosho did not remove the tree.

Much to his village's disappointment, Chief Osakwe tricked Bobo and sold the mill and all the other supplies to buyers in the regional capital of Kpolomo. He corrupted the orphan boy, Ebo, who had come from Ataku to help set up the mill and to show the Muvosho people how to operate it. Both worked together to dismantle the mill and haul it and all the supplies via a little-used path that led to Kpolomo. They sold all of it at cut-rate prices to crooked merchants. Ebo took his share of the money and fled to the capital city. Osakwe used a large part of his share to pay the dowry for a new wife and build a small house for her in his village. He also used part of the money to throw a big party in the village to pacify his people and make them overlook his gross wrongdoing.

At that party, he made a big speech. The final words of that speech went something like the following, "It is all right to steal from the white man. It is like stealing from the government. It is not the same as stealing from another person. We all know that thievery is the worst thing one can do, but stealing from foreigners or the government is not the same. It is not real thievery, especially as we know they are capable of replacing whatever they lose."

There was much grumbling among the villagers since Osakwe stole the mill the village needed so much. Even if it was not stealing, it was not his to take! As Bobo had well noted, Muvosho was the only village among the twenty villages in the District of Ataku without a mill to grind corn into the flour needed to prepare their major food staple. They were fed up with their chief and ready to take matters into their own hands before Bobo and other sprits struck their village with a mighty vengeance. They feared their chief's sins were so great that their entire village risked being wiped out.

A select group of village elders met quietly among themselves in a secluded opening in the surrounding bush. The village's head fetish priest led their discussions. He started each session with a prayer, asking for the forgiveness and compassion of Bobo, the grandfathers, and the spirits. They knew they needed to act fast if they were to avoid trouble with the other world. They could not delay demonstrating tangible and sincere remorse over what had happened. They had to do something quickly to save their village's honor and preserve it from destruction. After several clandestine meetings, the fetish priest said the grandfathers had communicated to him while he slept that they should not delay any longer in taking action. His stern and scary words propelled the people to act immediately.

Their plan was to arrest their chief and strip him of all his powers and wealth. Such a serious action was unprecedented in the historical annals of the village and the region. Nobody had heard of a chief being "destooled." Chief positions were for life, and they sat on their stools (thrones) until they died. Following a chief's death, it was usually one of his sons who replaced him. It was with much trepidation that a group of the strongest men in the village stormed into Osakwe's compound early the next morning and took him prisoner.

Osakwe's family was told to pack their things and leave the village by sundown. The chief was stood up, striped of his outer garments, and tightly tied to a tree in the center of the village. All the clan leaders and senior elders of the village encircled him. Behind those leaders were all of Muvosho's estimated two thousand inhabitants. The oldest man in the village approached Osakwe, insulted him, and spat on him. Osakwe did not react. He hung his head and closed his eyes, trying as hard as he could to numb his senses to the profound shock of the incredible disrespect he was being shown. Following the oldest man was the next oldest man, who treated Osakwe in the same rude manner. He was followed by every villager from the oldest to the youngest toddler. By the time they were finished, Osakwe was dying of shame. As saliva soiled every inch of his body, he was thinking of committing suicide at the first opportunity.

It was in that harsh, unheard of way that the villagers renounced their chief and demonstrated how much they thoroughly despised him and his ways. After all had finished paying the ultimate insult to their former chief, the senior elder asked everyone to sit on the ground while he pronounced the last words Osakwe would hear in his village. The old man took a deep breath as he searched for all the right words and the extra energy he needed to say them.

In an unsteady, aged voice, the old man said his words as firmly as he could, "Osakwe you are no longer our chief and we no longer know you or your family. Your theft of the grinding mill Bobo had so generously given us was an unforgivable sin against our village and grandfathers. We are obliged to treat you in this insulting way because we need to show Bobo and all those in the spirit world that we are truly sorry for what you did, and we are cutting all ties with you and your bad ways. From now on it is forbidden for your name to be mentioned in our village. We are doing this in the best interest of our village and its future. You must now leave the village and never come back. You are done here forever!"

As he shouted his last sentence with all his force, the old man stepped back in an exhausted state. Other men stepped forward and led Osakwe back to his compound. They allowed him to collect a few of his belongings and escorted him in silence out of the village, following the back path leading to Kpolomo. Two men followed Osakwe for the entire fifteen miles to Kpolomo to make sure he arrived. They also had the job of informing the traditional authorities in Kpolomo about Osakwe's 'destooling' and the reasons for it. They would travel on the next day to Ataku to deliver the same information to Chief Yofu, the superior chief of the district.

Before the sun set that day, the elders of Muvosho met and named one among them to serve as a regent until a new chief could be selected. They reconfirmed to themselves that the harsh punishment meted out to Osakwe was merited. They agreed unanimously that stripping him of his chiefly functions and banishing him from the village was extreme, but justified. They knew that banishment from one's village was the worst thing that could happen to anyone.

They also discussed the actions they needed to take as quickly as possible to appease Bobo and the spirit world. They decided they would send a team of men early the next day to work on removing the big tree that was blocking the road to Ataku. Once that was done, they would mobilize all the villagers to fix the road as the people of Ataku and other villages had already done. The big challenge they faced was how to replace the grinding mill. The cost of such a mill was beyond the collective resources of the village.

One elder came up with the idea of contacting all the people who had left their village to go live and work in Kpolomo or the capital city of Melomti. Many of those people had salaried jobs, and once the situation was explained to them they would be happy to make a contribution toward buying a grinding mill. They would know that, if they did not contribute to the grinding mill fund, they would not be warmly welcomed on their regular visits to the village.

The last thing anyone wanted was to be shown a poor welcome in his or her own village. They needed to visit their family members remaining in the village. When they became old they would retire to the village and be cared for by their community. All villagers living outside the village who were making money were expected to help their home village. People living outside the village wanted to be proud for how they helped their village and sought the prestige and respect that went with the assistance they provided to their village.

The elders estimated there were at least two hundred people from Muvosho living outside the village who had paying jobs. They calculated if each of those people gave the equivalent of ten dollars that would be enough money to buy and install a grinding mill. They were impressed by their own ingenuity in coming up with such a scheme, and they wondered why they had not done something like that before.

It was dawning on them that they could achieve much progress without external aid. If they really put their minds to it and they were unified in their desire to achieve a common objective, there was a lot they could do. For the first time, they were seeing that self-reliance and solidarity of purpose were good things. It became clear to them that they should stop waiting for outsiders and the government to come and do what they could do themselves. It was a moment of enlightenment! If they really wanted to improve the quality of their lives, there was much they could do themselves.

CHAPTER SIX
NATURAL INITIATION

Against their inner wishes, Celestine's parents rose early to accompany her to Atiwono's dumpy forest retreat. They were silent, but deep down their painful anxiety over what would happen to their daughter was tearing them apart. They had worked and sacrificed so their daughter would have a good life and now that effort was crumbling into dust. They grieved over that great loss and worried their spoiled daughter could not survive the poor and unsanitary conditions offered by Atiwono's humble encampment. Yet, they were helpless to do anything about their daughter's disturbing destiny. Sadly for them, Celestine's fate was sealed and their loss permanent.

With heavy hearts and a somber mood, they followed Celestine out the door of their compound to the path that led to Atiwono's earthly domain. While Celestine walked briskly ahead like a woman on a mission to achieve, her parents, confused and numb from the stress of the moment, dawdled and fell well behind her. When Celestine's parents arrived at Atiwono's compound, they were unable to find their daughter in the messy tangle of plants.

They stumbled about the compound and almost knocked over Atiwono who was sunk deeply into her wheelbarrow chaise. It was only after Atiwono made a grunting sound that they realized the wheelbarrow contained a living being. Atiwono followed her grunt with a weak spurt of welcoming words. The parents returned the greeting, but remained stone-faced.

It had been many years since either parent had ventured into Atiwono's domain. They were shocked by how it had fallen into a state of almost total ruin. Their immense pity for their daughter's fate plunged to even lower depths when they saw how much work would be involved with putting in acceptable order such an untidy domain. They were so overwhelmed by what they had observed they could not hear Atiwono talking to them. It was only when Atiwono belched out a loud burping sound that they focused their attention on her and bowed down to hear what she was trying to say.

As strongly as she could speak, Atiwono unevenly and haltingly emitted the following dramatic snippets, "Your daughter is now my daughter and the mother-to-be of my plant world. She has been called by the plant spirits to replace me, and they are counting on her to work diligently to represent them on this Earth. The end of my time is near. There is no time to lose."

Chief Gyasi swallowed hard upon hearing those words and said in a low and troubled voice, "We are hurting deeply, but we understand the will of the other world must prevail. All we ask is to see Celestine one more time to say good-bye."

Like the croaking of an out-of-breath frog, Atiwono replied, "Celestine is no more. There is only Atibona who will ensure my legacy after I am gone. Please leave the things you have brought and return home. Do not worry. You will see in time that all is for the best for all concerned. Do not speak of this to anyone and do not come back until you are summoned. Thank you."

Chief Gyasi was visibly shaken by Atiwono's final words and his wife was sobbing. The unexpected news about not seeing their daughter before leaving added to their agony. They were not prepared to go home without saying good-bye. There were things they wanted to discuss with their daughter before separating from her, but now that would not be possible. In particular, her mother wanted to discuss a few things in private with Celestine. Her mother suspected Celestine was pregnant and she wanted to ask her about that. They regretted that they had not kept up with their daughter and spoken with her before she entered Atiwono's compound. Their daughter was now lost to them and they were suffering profoundly from an ugly mixture of grief and anger. They could not understand why life was being so unfair to them.

Their despondency was total and their lives had changed forever. They would never get over the sacrifice of their daughter for the good of the spirit world and all the people of the District of Ataku. They were prostrate with grief and unable to tell their neighbors and family in the village the reason for their mourning. Some villagers thought their daughter had run away to join a man in a distant town and that misfortune was too shameful for her parents to admit. They could not explain what had happened to their daughter and, even if they wanted to, they were prohibited from talking about their daughter's unfathomable new situation. They acted as if they did not care what people said about their daughter. They knew that in time all would be revealed to everyone, but until then, it would remain their deeply buried secret.

After her parents left Atiwono's compound, Atibona stepped out of a modest daub and wattle dwelling that stood in an overgrown corner of the compound, dressed in a new multicolored gown that Atiwono had been saving for years to give to her replacement. That gown, like the old and very tattered one worn by Atiwono, was made of many scraps of cloth remnants sown together. Atibona detested wearing such a gown, as it was of the sort only poor old women wore. Yet, there was clearly a bright glow around her. In that gown, in that place, and in her new role she had taken on a completely new aura. As much as Atiwono's scrunched up face allowed, she smiled when she saw Atibona. Her frail body swelled with happiness.

Atibona stood silently by, peering down at Atiwono's pitiful state, and asking herself if she would end up the same way at the end of her life. Atiwono called the young man, Leon, who had been serving as her caretaker, and dismissed him, telling him not to come back unless he would be called by Atibona. From that point until her last breath, Atibona would care for her. Atiwono had to focus on transferring as much knowledge as possible about the plant world to Atibona before she passed on to the other world. No other human could be present while Atibona did her apprenticeship. All the secrets Atiwono would reveal to Atibona were for her eyes and ears only.

As soon as Leon exited the compound, Atiwono began Atibona's initiation. She started by telling her all about the plants around her and continued with different plants growing in her compound. Atibona pushed Atiwono along in her wheelbarrow in a concentric manner from the nearest to the farthest plants, stopping repeatedly to hear Atiwono's description of each plant, their uses and powers. She explained in detail the prayers to say to each plant spirit before harvesting the plants and how to prepare and apply them. Before leaving each plant, Atiwono would ask Atibona to repeat what she had said and to commit every word she uttered to memory.

Atiwono delighted in revealing the properties of each plant. She would lovingly caress each plant, call out its name, and generally say something like the following: "This plant is used for indigestion. You must dry its leaves for five days and then grind them in a small mortar into a fine powder that can be sprinkled on food. To keep this plant thriving you must prune its bottom leaves, keep the ground around it clear of other plants, and make sure it has sufficient water. As the sprits have called you to this vocation, you must bless each plant before anyone takes them to the village for distribution. You need to explain to your assistant how the medicine is to be administered. You must not ever ask for any compensation, and you can only accept payment through your assistant from people who have benefited from your medicinal plants. I suggest that you keep my caretaker, Leon, as your assistant until you find one of your own. Leon is trustworthy and he already knows the work that must be done."

Atibona was impressed by the long list of ailments plants could alleviate. Atiwono had plants that could cure hypertension, headaches, malaria, asthma, fever, depression, epilepsy, venereal diseases, gout, and various infections. The list was almost endless. Atibona was surprised to find she had a good memory for that kind of information and was impressed by her heretofore unknown ability in that arcane field of traditional knowledge. Atiwono was pleased to see how Atibona took quickly and firmly to the subject. Atibona's uncanny ability in that domain confirmed for Atiwono that she was indeed her chosen successor.

Each day they repeated the same circular tour until Atibona could repeat, without making any mistakes, everything Atiwono had told her about each plant. After a few days, Atiwono asked Atibona to recite from memory the names, properties, uses, and the processes employed to manipulate each plant and its spirit. That recitation took almost two hours. Atibona was so flawless in her presentation that Atiwono wept as her heart pounded with much joy. Adding to the eeriness was the stillness and silence of the myriad of birds and cats in the compound. It was as if they too were judging the competency of their new master.

Atibona was so preoccupied with all she had to learn that she had forgotten about time and the sordid conditions in which she lived. Indeed, she was captivated and fully absorbed by her new life, and in an odd way she was pleased that her life had become important and meaningful. Previously, she was a pretty chief's daughter, but she had become the new mother of all plants and guardian of their secrets. Nobody knew what she knew. She understood the high importance of her knowledge and new role as a traditional healer. Her dreaded fate appeared to be a blessing in disguise. She was beginning to accept her new situation as her true calling in life. There was no turning back. No matter what, she would always be the mother of plants for the rest of her life.

She felt reborn and began to appreciate that she was chosen for that exalted duty. As her contentment with her changed circumstances grew, she stopped caring about all the deprivations she endured by living poor in Atiwono's bush compound. She learned to live simply and only with the basics. Her diet consisted of corn mush made from the bags of flour people left at the entry to their compound as charitable donations and payment for the medicines they used. Atiwono showed her how to prepare a sauce from the leaves of plants growing in and around the compound to accompany the mush. They used water from an artesian well that trickled from under a boulder next to their compound. Atibona lost much weight and her body changed in size and form. Nobody who knew her before would recognize her now. As mirrors were prohibited in the plant world, Atibona was not able to know how her face had also changed.

One bodily change that remained constant for Atibona was the baby growing inside her, making her abdomen bulge. She called Atiwono's attention to the baby growing in her womb and the need to gain the recognition of Bobo for his child. Atiwono grunted her assent and said, "I know very well that you have a baby boy growing in your stomach and this boy needs to be joined by his father."

"How do you know I am carrying a boy child?" expressed a surprised Atibona.

"The plants and trees have repeated many times that your child is a boy. To complete your new powers, you, too, must learn quickly to hear what the living organisms around you are saying," Atiwono blurted out in an unusually clear manner.

"I agree. I must learn to hear the plants. How do I do that?" inquired Atibona.

Atiwono replied briefly, "Tomorrow we will start working on that."

Early the next day Atiwono said, "You have learned all there is to know of what is inside the compound. Now, take me outside the compound to continue your learning."

They repeatedly circled the compound in an ever-widening circumference. Every time they encountered a new plant, bush, or tree, Atiwono would follow the same process she had done inside the compound. She communicated as clearly as she could all there was to know about each organic being and asked Atibona to recite what she had said. They did that over and over for several days until Atibona had all the necessary information firmly embedded in her mind.

When that last stage of the learning process was complete, Atiwono turned her head and looked for a long time at Atibona, who waited patiently to hear what Atiwono would say next. Atiwono finally said in a soft but firm voice, "You are ready."

"Ready for what?" begged Atibona.

"Ready to listen to the plants talking and replace me," Atiwono chuckled happily.

"I am listening, but I do not hear the plants saying anything," Atibona affirmed indignantly.

Atiwono insisted, "Listen harder! Close your eyes and repeat your name and say their new mother is calling to them."

Atibona did as Atiwono instructed. She concentrated with all her might and repeated over and over her call to the plants. When she was almost ready to give up, she suddenly heard a multitude of whispers flowing into her head, filling her ears with a cacophony of strange voices speaking in various dialects. Her head was immediately busting with more words than she could handle, making it impossible to understand what was being said.

"Mama Atiwono, I can hear! I can hear so very much!" Atibona exclaimed with joy at the top of her voice. Atibona said, "Mama Atiwono, please help me. There is much I do not understand and there are too many voices speaking at once."

When she received no reply from Atiwono, she opened her eyes and looked down at the wheelbarrow to see if she was going to reply or not. Atibona was shocked by what she saw. Mama Atiwono was not in the wheelbarrow! All that was left in the wheelbarrow was her old and much soiled multicolored gown. Mama Atiwono was gone! She had been taken by the spirit world in a twinkling of an eye. Her time had come at the very moment the other world was certain Atibona was the one who could indeed replace her. As the spirit world can only communicate with one human on Earth, Mama Atiwono had to leave Earth before Atibona could hear the plants talk. Atibona was frightened and rolled the wheelbarrow quickly back to the compound. She was overcome by the rapid departure of Atiwono. She felt very much alone. It was a frightening moment for her. That was the first time in her life she had been alone.

Atibona sat down on a log and took some deep breaths as she tried to calm herself and size up her solitary situation. After a while, she felt surprisingly at peace. She realized she was not alone. The birds and cats were there, and more importantly, hundreds of plants were there to keep her company. If there was a strong need to do so, she knew Atiwono would find a way to communicate with her from the other world. She was concerned that Atiwono left before she could tell her how to go about getting Bobo back. She thought that Atiwono might see Bobo in the spirit world and learn more about how to bring him back to an earthly life. She told herself to be alert for any unusual signs.

In the following days, Atibona focused on listening to the plants and trying to understand them. She also wanted to see if they could hear and understand her. She made a huge effort to sort out which plant was talking and how to call on an individual plant. That was a mammoth task and she could see it would take years to master plant languages and sort out all the communication patterns used by each plant. She was forcing herself to learn as much as possible quickly because she needed to find a way to talk to the ancient baobab that had consumed Bobo before the birth of her baby. For her, it was a race against time. She believed the life of her baby depended on the success of her efforts to recover Bobo.

CHAPTER SEVEN
MAKING WRONGS RIGHT

Chiefs Yofu and Gyasi were ensnared in a quandary from which they could not see any exit. With their most senior advisors gathered around them, Chief Yofu declared in a mournful tone, "We are pleased with the positive changes occurring in our villages, but we are also deeply tormented by what remains to be done. We are overwhelmed by the daunting challenges facing us."

Chief Gyasi quickly and pointedly added, "There is much to do to make right the wrongs each village has committed against the other. We know we will be eternally condemned if we cannot redress the wrongs our ancient feud has caused us to commit against one another."

They knew Bobo was profoundly disturbed over the destruction by the people of Aniko of the school he helped build in Ataku. If they could not correct that egregious "wrong" Bobo had suffered during his time with them, they would be forever cursed. None of their other good works could ever compensate for that dastardly deed. They had to find a way to rebuild the school Bobo had generously helped build.

The chiefs spent much of their time discussing and reflecting on how they could obtain the resources needed to rebuild the primary school in Ataku. They examined repeatedly all the options, but could not find a way to collect the resources needed.

Lamenting their thorny predicament, Chief Yofu spoke forcefully, "To rebuild the school, we must obtain as much money as possible from our brethren living in the capital city and other towns. But, even if they all gave as much as they could, it would still not be enough to cover all the costs of reconstructing the school. We can provide the labor, sand, gravel, and water needed, but we cannot raise sufficient funds to buy the cement, rebar, roofing material, and other accessories that must be bought from stores in the regional capital of Kpolomo. How and where can we obtain the approximate two thousand dollars required to buy the needed supplies?"

While the chiefs were preoccupied with the school money issue, villagers kept seeking ways to improve themselves and their living conditions. There were daily meetings of various work committees in the villages to discuss and determine which activities they could implement that would result in improvements. There was the roads and paths committee as well as different committees for water, sanitation, health, nutrition, literacy, and education. Each committee had an elected leader and a literate secretary who could take notes on their meetings. They applied a very participatory process, where men and women were represented and had an equal say in matters. Their discussions were lively, and sometimes unanimous agreement was not achieved. Contentious issues were decided by a showing of hands. A majority vote ruled.

It was obvious that governance mechanisms in the villages were also improving.

The sanitation committee in charge of village cleanliness set up a system for sweeping the village and disposing of all waste material. Huge trash collection baskets were placed at various locations throughout the villages. Those baskets were emptied at regular intervals by rotating groups of sanitation committee members, and their contents were taken to designated village dumps located a good distance to the east of the villages. Those dumps had been fenced in, and two very deep rectangular holes had been dug for the disposal of waste.

Another subcommittee was in charge of sorting out the trash, placing organic material in one hole and nonorganic in another hole. The former hole was for creating compost that could be used later as a natural fertilizer on farmers' fields. After years of cultivating the same land without adding any fertilizer and using the same slash and burn method of cultivation, the land had been depleted of the organic matter needed for crop growth. Crop yields had declined steadily over the years, making it harder for people to feed the fast-growing number of additional mouths.

A system of fines was put in place to penalize anyone discarding trash outside the trash collection baskets. Each compound was instructed to install a family trash basket so that hygienic conditions within the compounds would improve. Each family was also encouraged to have its own compost pit for the dumping of waste and any animal manure. People were also urged to tether or cage their animals in one place so as to facilitate manure collection and improve animal feeding and care practices. They selected knowledgeable leaders to show people how to make compost and spread it on their gardens and fields to enrich the soil and, thereby, to increase yields.

The joint superior council of the villages was contemplating prohibiting marauding animals in each village, thus requiring animals within the villages to be tethered, fenced in, or caged. Otherwise, it was highly recommended that people keep their animals outside of the village on their farmland. One other challenge facing hygienic improvements in the villages was children defecating and peeing everywhere. Families were instructed to clean up after their children and dispose of their excrement in their compound pit latrines.

The sanitation committee found that those measures were a good start, but not sufficient to achieve their goal of one hundred percent village cleanliness. They were concerned about all diseases transmitted by the excess of flies in the village. They knew that most people defecated at designated places in the nearby outskirts of their villages and that flies could easily feed in those areas, and then contaminate food and water consumed by humans. The only solution they could envisage for that important health problem was to oblige each compound to construct a family pit latrine.

That was not an easy solution to apply. Digging a proper family pit latrine was a major undertaking that required much labor, skill, and money. A model latrine was constructed in the chief's compound and people were invited to see how it was built and maintained. A representative of each compound was trained in how to dig a latrine to the desired ten-foot depth, cover it, and build a small earthen block outhouse around it, placing a thatch roof on its top. If desired, a tin door could be installed for the latrine stall or a cloth could be hung on the doorway to permit privacy.

Separate latrine stalls for women and men were encouraged. The importance of building latrines downhill and distant from any water sources was stressed. The need to install a plastic or bamboo pipe for the aeration of the pit was also emphasized, as was the need to keep the latrine stall clean and the latrine hole covered with a wood plank when it was not in use.

For weeks people were busy building their family latrines. The few shovels and pick axes in the villages were passed from one compound to another. Much work was involved, as it was difficult to dig in the rock-hard laterite soil. People were proud of their finished latrines, and they would invite their neighbors to visit and use their latrines. There was active competition as each family tried to build and make their latrine better than the ones built by their neighbors. The sanitation committee decided to hold a contest whereby a select group of elders would judge the merits of each latrine. The winner of that contest would be awarded two sheets of galvanized tin roofing to cover his or her home latrine and make a door for it. The people jokingly called that award the "shithouse prize."

The people were very proud of the hundreds of family latrines built in their villages and wryly declared their villages to be the cleanest in the country. The word of that exceptional achievement traveled far and wide and it was not long before people were coming from other villages to see what had been achieved in Ataku and Aniko. Visitors were very impressed with what they saw, and said they would return to their home villages and try to undertake the same hygienic measures. The chiefs of Ataku and Aniko were very proud that what they had achieved in their villages was being replicated in many other villages. That kind of positive "spin-off" was something they had not anticipated.

The chiefs were particularly proud because their achievements were accomplished without the use of any outside assistance. They were finding that maximum self-reliance was a good policy to follow and they were committed to making as many improvements as they could without the use of any outside assistance. They wanted the destinies of their two villages to be fully in their hands and not dependent on external aid. They believed it was entirely up to them to elaborate a development strategy tailored to fit their particular circumstances.

The number of people, including foreigners from the capital city of Melomti, coming to the village increased. That large number of visitors represented something of an economic boom for the villages as they spent money on food and other items in the villages. So many visitors were stopping by Chez Andre's for food and refreshments that he used the extra income to refurbish and expand his bar and restaurant. He also added items to his food and drink menu. Those improvements resulted in further increases in customers, particularly white foreigners from the capital city.

The wood carvers who lived and worked on the outskirts of Ataku set up a small shop and work place near Chez Andre's so they could cater to the increasing number of visitors. Women also cleared and covered a place across the road from Chez Andre's to sell their wares to the visitors. Some women groups formed to make curios and traditional clothes they sold to the visitors.

All visitors were very impressed with how clean the villages were and said they would tell their friends to come and see for themselves what had been achieved. They expressed their high appreciation of the nicely maintained road leading to the villages. They noted how pleasing it was to see how the roadsides were kept clear of brush and that whitewashed stones had been placed along both sides of the road. They also had favorable comments about the decorative sign the villages had erected at the edge of the main road. They were pleased that the attractive sign clearly indicated where to turn off the main road to go to Ataku and Aniko. (Or, "Atakuniko," as some visitors called the villages.)

Many of those visitors wanted to see the chiefs and their compounds. The chiefs decided to fix up part of Chief Yofu's compound in a very authentic style and perform musical and dancing presentations for visitors, as well as some retelling of village history and folklore. The number of visitors coming to the chief's compound became so high that the two chiefs would take turns meeting visitors. Those visits required that Chief Gyasi break with his customary business dress and drape himself in traditional African clothes like Chief Yofu always wore. Many villagers also dressed in their best traditional clothes on a daily basis, as they never knew when a group of visitors would arrive.

The people were happy to receive so many visitors, but after a while, catering to those visitors became a lot of work. The number of visitors overwhelmed the chiefs, who realized that they needed some kind of system in place to control their number. They also resolutely believed that system should result in greater income for their villages, especially as they needed additional income to undertake a variety of village improvement projects. After consulting with their elders and clan leaders, and offering libations to the grandfathers and Bobo, they decided to set up modest toll collection booths at the entrances to their villages. The toll amount would be very small, and if anyone objected strongly to its payment, he or she would still be allowed to pass.

The chiefs were surprised that nobody objected to the toll, and sometimes white foreigners gave more money than they needed to pay. Many visitors seemed eager to help the village to achieve its development objectives. A short presentation was prepared for use by those collecting the toll so the visitors would know the money collected would go to the villages' development fund and for the building of a new primary school. That kind of sales pitch worked very well and the amount of money in the villages' development fund coffer grew rapidly.

A well-respected elderly man, who had worked previously in the city as an accountant, was selected as the villages' treasurer. One of his first acts was to ask for a room in Chief Yofu's compound to use as an office and to gain permission to use some of the funds already collected to buy supplies and a safe for the keeping of the money. The main task of that man was to make sure all monies were collected and written records were kept of all income and expenditures. The creation of that new position represented something of a breakthrough for the villages, which were on a fast-moving learning curve. The chiefs and their subjects were learning many new things and one of those things was that local revenue generation and competent management of funds collected were critical to being in control of their development process and self-governing plans.

A new committee was established to organize tours of the villages and the surrounding countryside, including special climbs up to the top of Mount Ataku. Visitors were all too ready to pay a fee for those tours. As many visitors complained that one day in a village was not enough, the superior council decided to offer room and board in selected compounds for visitors who wanted to experience African life. That program became so popular that all families wanted to participate, fixing up their compounds so as to be eligible for the novel "live-in" program.

Families derived many benefits from that program. Solid human relationships were forged between villagers and the visitors staying in their compound. Many visitors returned repeatedly to stay with what they called their village family. Each time they came, they bore gifts and were always helping their African families with their financial needs. Some visitors would take some children to live with them in the capital and invite their village families to come and visit them.

Those exchange visits were not only helpful financially, but also worked to open the villagers' horizons in terms of learning how things were in other parts of the world. That exposure to the outside world helped open their minds to innovations and improving their circumstances. They could see that a long-term "marriage" between their families and those from other countries was a very good thing and supportive of their desire for progress. The villagers shared everything they knew with their visitors except for some quasi-secret traditions and Bobo's story, which had to remain their secret.

The people were happy with the progress they had achieved and all the changes occurring in their villages. Adapting to those changes was not easy for everyone, particularly the older people, and there were some complaints. People complained that keeping their animals in one place was too difficult to do, as it required extra work in terms of bringing feed and water to the animals. Things were much easier when animals could scavenge on their own for food. Some mothers also complained that it was too hard to follow their children everywhere and clean up after them. Other people complained that making compost and spreading it on their fields was too much work.

It was obvious that the changes required in many routines entailed added labor but those adaptations represented part of the price of achieving progress. The chiefs insisted the villagers had to work harder and be more disciplined if they wanted to get ahead. They knew it was a time for making tough choices, but choices had to be made if their villages were ever to achieve lasting progress. The chiefs were fond of saying, "If we are to please Bobo and improve our situation, we must change our mindset and work ethic. We are convinced that the desired transformation of our impoverished circumstances requires all villagers to transcend themselves. A fundamental and permanent change in our human nature is necessary if we are to get ahead and stay ahead."

The people understood that, but found it very hard to change their nature and traditional ways of doing things. They were proud of all they had achieved and much happier than they were before the secret transformation of Bobo. They could see their achievements had resulted in improvements in their lives, but they remained too poor and often ill from scourges like malaria. Many times they did not have enough to eat, and the lack of diversity in their diets did not permit good nutrition. Particularly, too many children were still malnourished.

People pondered out loud, "What good will all our efforts make if we remain desperately poor and badly nourished and often sick? Far too many infants continue to die, as do many mothers while giving birth. Much of the extra money earned from visitors goes to buying more food and paying medical bills. We work very hard, but even if we work harder we have little to show for our labors. Prices for the essential items we need continue to rise and the money we have buys less than before. We feel powerless and mired in a debilitating poverty trap."

At the very least, they needed the kind of prosperity that brought less hunger and more income. For them, having a consistent supply of good food and money in their pockets was what brought happiness and more hope for a better future. But there were so many important factors beyond their control and comprehension. There were also too many "unpredictable" issues that made it almost impossible to plan and anticipate where they should devote their efforts.

The chiefs knew they had their work cut out for them. They could easily see there was much more to do and many more miles to travel on the self-improvement journey before their people would turn the corner and be on a firm, self-perpetuating upward development track. The more they were able to achieve, the more they saw there was more yet to do. They knew they had to be courageous and steadfast if they were to stay the course over the long haul on the desired development course. They realized it took many years of constant and well-focused effort in a peaceful and stable environment to get ahead and stay ahead. They had to be committed to staying the course over the long run if the positive changes required to perpetuate and multiply progress from one generation to another were to occur.

Achieving a better and permanent way forward was such a daunting challenge that the villagers prayed for the help of the spirit world and the grandfathers. Most of all, they asked Bobo to support them and intervene on their behalf in the other world. They beseeched Bobo for his understanding and wise guidance. They knew that all they were achieving was because of Bobo, and they needed his support to succeed. They feared they could not live up to Bobo's high expectations. Deep down they felt incapable of changing their own basic nature to the extent needed to move them to a higher and much better level of development.

CHAPTER EIGHT
THE KANSAS CONNECTION

O n the other side of the world, in faraway Kansas, a different kind of drama was unfolding. J.B. was sick. He had suffered from an agitated state during the last full moon, and he was having trouble taking his morning walks. As people watched him go by they could see his step was not as lively and brisk as before. He took much longer to complete his daily walk and he struggled to do his daily rounds. J.B. appeared as if he had aged many years in just a few months. He had become weak and decrepit. His back had developed a small hunch and he was so stooped that he was now very short. People could see J.B. had become very frail, and they tried to keep a close eye on him in case he needed medical attention. All feared that J.B.'s days on the Earth were coming to an end, and they were not sure which actions they should take.

J.B. had ceased, long ago, of being capable of any logical thought processes. His every action was governed by innate instincts. He was totally at the mercy of involuntary reactions to his surroundings. He had forgotten why he took his morning walk in the manner he did and why he danced in the light of the full moon. He had become a creature of nature and habit. He had become part of the natural environment and moved according to the moon, stars, and wind. The only voices he heard were from his plants and his distant past in Africa. His inner being was in tune to the beating of African drums that called him nonstop to return to the village he had left behind many years ago. The only word he muttered was one nobody could understand. Once, a child who had approached J.B. heard him saying repeatedly in a low voice a strange word, "abakoo." In reality, J.B. was saying "Ataku," the name of the village in Africa where he had lived many years ago.

One bright morning nobody saw J.B. pass by to go on his morning walk. As that had never happened before, people became alarmed. The night before, there was a brilliant flash of light that some of J.B.'s neighbors noted but, as it happened so quickly and nothing changed, they paid no mind. Some people thought it was a random bolt of lightning on the plains after a hot summer day. Nobody could possibly make the connection between that instantaneous flash of light and the occurrence of the full moon. That unusual flash of light the night before was quickly forgotten as the unsettling word spread in the community that J.B. had not taken his morning walk. Panic engulfed the community and a search party composed of his closest neighbors was organized to look for him. Some people feared that he had been struck by a bolt of lightning.

Every inch of J.B.'s path was examined for any clues that could provide information on his whereabouts. Two members of the search party waded through the stream that J.B. always knelt at to make sure he had not fallen into the water. They circumvented every part of J.B.'s yard surrounding his small house. They could not find anything that gave them any clues about where J.B. could be. The only thing left to do was to search inside his house. Doing that would require involving the city police and fire department. One of the search party members sped off to alert the local authorities and enlist the support of the police to enter J.B.'s room. In the meantime, food was brought to feed J.B.'s numerous cats and fish, which were racing around in groups in clockwise circles. Even after food was brought, the cats kept racing nonstop around the house in a big circle, one after another in some relentless pursuit of an invisible prey. The goldfish in their little pond were doing the same. People became dizzy after watching the amazing spectacle for some time. Others became frightened and fled to the safety of their homes.

It was late afternoon before the police and firemen arrived with the court order they needed to break into J.B.'s room. They knocked open J.B.'s private door and were prepared to rush in, but the awful smell that poured out of J.B.'s room had them scurrying backward with their hands over their eyes and noses. That indescribable rotten smell indicated only one thing: J.B. had died and his remains were emitting the worst odor anyone had ever experienced in their lives. The police feared there were contaminants that could spread. They cordoned off J.B.'s house, ordering the crowd that had gathered to go home. The police could see that special sanitation equipment would be needed to go into J.B.'s room and recover his remains.

Nightfall was fast approaching and special lighting was set up to permit city workers to continue with their work at J.B.'s house. Sanitation workers arrived, as did the city coroner. Two men were chosen to enter the house. They put on protective garments, gloves, and rubber boots. They also wore surgical masks scented with a minty air freshener. Lights were aimed to shine through J.B.'s door and the men entering J.B.'s tiny inner sanctum carried powerful flashlights. The electricity to the house had been cut off long ago. The men carefully entered J.B.'s room, moving slowly to avoid the incredible amount of debris that covered the concrete floor. There was rotting vegetative matter everywhere, as all the plants J.B. kept had died long ago. The small bird and lizard cages he had built and hung from the ceiling were full of decaying remains. The men could not believe the mess. They did not know how anyone could live in such unhygienic, filthy conditions.

J.B.'s miniature room made it easy for the men to conclude quickly that there was not a human body in the room. The only place a body could have been was under an old shabby quilt spread over a worn and very soiled mattress on the floor; but when that quilt was pulled back only a mouse's nest was found. J.B.'s remains were definitely not in his room. The men were forced to leave the room. They could no longer tolerate the unbearable smell generated by the rotten plants and dead birds and lizards. The confines of J.B.'s stale, windowless room had bred a cesspool of disease. Nothing of any real value was observed in the room. The city authorities ordered all the contents of J.B.'s room to be removed and taken to the city incinerator for immediate burning. Once the room had been scrapped clean of its contents, it was to be scrubbed with a powerful lye detergent. J.B.'s house would remain cordoned off until it was certain there was no longer any sanitary threat.

It took several hours before all those nauseous cleansing actions could be completed. It was almost midnight before the sanitation crew and city authorities completed their work. The city mayor, Mr. Peabody, came to verify that everything had been done as instructed. He was satisfied with what he saw, and he was about to tell everyone to pack up and go home when he noticed there was still a strange smell coming from the house. As J.B.'s room smelled of industrial strength disinfectant, there was only one place from which such a bad smell could emanate. It had to be coming from the remaining part of the small ramshackle house that was occupied by J.B.'s older brother and his sister-in-law. When police questioned neighbors about the elderly couple, they said they had not been seen in many years. The entire neighborhood thought they had moved away a long time ago and left the place to the eccentric J.B.

Mayor Peabody ordered the search of the other side of the house. That part of the house was tightly shuttered, and its one door was firmly closed and locked. The curtains were fully closed, preventing any peering through the three small windows. The fire department wasted no time breaking open the door. The same procedures used to search J.B.'s isolated room were employed. Sanitation agents in their protective gear slowly entered the house while searchlights were trained on the door opening. Upon entry they found themselves in a small kitchenette that was very tidy except for the thick layer of dust and musty soot that covered everything. A small, modestly furnished sitting room adjoined that area. The agents shined their lights on the drab wallpaper that was peeling off the walls. There was nothing on the walls except one small black and white photo in an oval wooden frame of a young couple. The agents surmised it was a photo of J.B.'s brother and his sister-in-law when they were married over a half-century ago.

A lonely old vertical dial phone stood on a small end table with its cable dangling off to one side. There was a faded and threadbare loveseat on one side of the tiny room and next to it was a matching wing chair turned in the opposite direction. The agents carefully walked across the cheap worn carpet to see if anything was on the other side of the sofa and wing chair. The first agent to arrive at the other side of the wing chair was stopped in his tracks by a horrifying sight. He let out a loud moaning cry and waved to his co-worker to come see what was in the wing chair. Sitting in the chair was a corpse dressed in a tattered dress that was fashionable forty years ago. The corpse had brittle patches of dried brown skin sticking on its skeletal frame. The corpse looked like it had been freeze-dried; its remaining flesh was pulled tight against the bones. The skull had a small, bemusing, but impertinent smile. Clutched in the corpse's bony hands was an old dog-eared copy of a much worn King James Bible. The putrid smell of death had long since been absorbed by the shabby environs of the homely tomb.

After encountering that haunting scene, the agents were eager to finish their inspection and leave the nightmarish house. They knew that before they could report to those waiting outside they needed to inspect the small bedroom adjoining the sitting room. They opened very slowly the old undersized wooden door to the bedroom. The door made an eerie creaking noise that raised their level of anxiety. The tiny room was very dark. They shined their flashlights through the partially opened door and saw that the room was almost entirely filled with an old metal-frame double bed. They opened the door wider and one man reluctantly stepped into the room and swept his flashlight quickly around the room. His light passed quickly over the bed and he noticed something that made him slowly return the beam of his flashlight to the bed. He aimed his light at the head of the bed to see a startling sight. His hand shook as he peered at the head of another shriveled corpse. The head seemed to be peeking out of the top of the soiled quilted bed cover.

That was enough for him. He quickly backed out of the room and called in a frightened voice to his colleague. "Let's get the hell out of this house from hell!" They both ran for the exit so fast that they stumbled into the group waiting for them outside.

Mayor Peabody demanded, "What is going on? Why are you trembling and acting like a couple of scared children?"

The men sat on the ground and tried to calm themselves enough to say some words that made sense. In a halting, choked manner one man managed to say the word, "corpses."

The mayor took the man by the shoulders and shook him. He looked straight into his eyes and asked forcefully in a loud voice, "What are you talking about, son? Get a hold of yourself and tell us what you saw! Come on now. Stop your blithering nonsense and give us a report that we can act on."

After some minutes, the other man said softly, as if talking to himself, "There are two bodies in the house. They have been dead for a long time." After saying those words he fainted and dropped flat onto the ground. His colleague placed him alongside his fallen comrade.

With a distorted look of worry and puzzlement, Mayor Peabody repeated in a squeaky, high-pitched voice what the man had said. Upon hearing those words, the group was temporarily stunned into silence. It took the mayor some minutes to regain his composure and tell the chief of police, "This is now a matter for the state police. Please call them immediately and tell them to get their butts over here at top speed!" The chief of police ran off with a couple of his colleagues and jumped into his nearby police car from where he radioed the state police. It was almost dawn before the first contingent of three state police investigators arrived. They quickly donned their protective gear and entered the rickety old house with their huge flashlights. They made a full inventory of everything in the house and recorded a detailed description of the two corpses. Later, a special forensics team joined them, took many photographs, and gently bagged the corpses for further examination in their lab. They took down the testimonies of all who were there and over the next several days they asked many questions of all the neighbors. Their on-site work lasted to almost noon, but it would take days to complete their final report.

Their final report dryly concluded that the two corpses were of the elderly married couple that the neighbors thought had moved away years ago. They had both died nearly at the same time of natural causes. The man died first in his bed and was covered up by his wife who later sat down in her easy chair to wait for death. She died a few days later. Before the woman died, she had cleaned and arranged everything in their humble dwelling. No note or anything was left to explain the mystery of their deaths. Moreover, there were not any clues to indicate the whereabouts of J.B., who had almost been forgotten about in all the commotion surrounding the discovery of the desiccated remains of his older brother and sister-in-law.

The occurrence of that amazing event in the small town of Gemini, Kansas, made the national news. The police released an all-points bulletin on the missing J.B. Surprisingly, nobody had a photo of his face. People said J.B. did not like his photo taken so they had prohibited people from taking his photo. The people of Gemini collected money and offered a $5,000 reward to anyone with information on the whereabouts of J.B., their town folk hero. People in Gemini were befuddled by his sudden disappearance and ashamed because they had never noticed the passing of his brother and sister-in-law. Their eyes were always focused on what J.B. was doing and no attention was paid to the aged brother and his wife. Mayor Peabody was quoted as saying, "How can two citizens of our town die, and be dead for so long without anyone noticing anything amiss? They were recluses who did not want to be bothered, but they did not deserve to die in this way."

Mayor Peabody declared a day of mourning for the couple, arranged a memorial service, and a decent burial in the city cemetery. A special tombstone was set atop their burial plot, noting that J.B.'s brother and sister-in-law were buried there. People were embarrassed because they did not know their names or J.B.'s real name. They also did not know their birth or death dates. They only noted the date on the tombstone their bodies were discovered and that they had died peacefully at home. One brave soul placed an obituary in the city newspaper saying much of the same thing, adding they were longtime residents of the community and had left behind a beloved brother, J.B., who was a well-known local folk hero. A reproduction of the marriage photo found on the wall in their living room was placed with the obituary in the newspaper. People wanted everyone to see that they were once real people and a lovely couple.

Once all the evidence had been gleaned from the ancient little run-down house and yard where J.B. lived, the city authorities decided the house should be bulldozed and the remaining debris hauled to the city landfill. The house was about to fall down anyway; it was designated a health hazard and unfit for human occupation. In the house's place would be erected a concrete monument in the memory of J.B., and the yard would be turned into a neighborhood park. A contest would be held for designs of a J.B. monument. J.B.'s goldfish were sold at a very high price to a tropical fish store, which promised to continue to raise that special breed of goldfish. There was already a long waiting list to buy descendants of J.B.'s goldfish. The sales pitch for those goldfish was "Keep J.B.'s Spirit Alive, Buy J.B. Goldfish."

The same happened at a local pet store that provided a new home for J.B.'s cats and sold their offspring to the highest bidder. The slogan of that store was "Buy a J.B. Cat and Be One with the Full Moon." Both stores agreed to give 15 percent of their earnings on the sale of J.B. goldfish and cats to the J.B. Memorial Fund, which the town would use to build his monument, and equip and maintain the J.B. Neighborhood Park. Any funds remaining would be used to hire private investigators to continue to solve the mystery of J.B.'s sudden disappearance without a trace. Also, funds were used to hire a professional writer to document J.B.'s life and write a book about him and the influence he had on the town of Gemini.

Weeks after all the commotion had ended and things had settled down, there was never a day that went by without people asking, "What happened to J.B.? How could he leave us without any forewarning? Not even a word! Our lives are so empty and dull without J.B.! How could he do this to us?"

Little did they know that J.B. was the happiest he had been in his life. After years of waiting, he had finally been lifted up by a moonbeam flash and transported to the spirit world in the African village he was forced to leave over a decade ago. The people did not know that miraculous event was what had always dominated J.B.'s life. He had focused his entire being on using his connection with the power of the full moon to return to his African home. They also did not know that the zigzag pattern of the path made by his morning walk was the rough shape of the five points of a baobab tree leaf. All J.B. wanted was to go back to the old baobab that had mysteriously consumed him many years ago in Africa. He knew he could only find peace and his final resting place within that ancient baobab tree. The people of Gemini would never know the true story of their wacky town folk hero whose legend continued to grow larger than reality with each passing day.

CHAPTER NINE
TREE TALK

Celestine progressively became shrouded by a bright aura that made her look like an angel. The more she sensed her deep contentment with her new position in life the more she glowed. She had adapted fully to being Mama Atiwono's replacement for all things related to plants and trees. Her full surrender to her new calling gave profound meaning to her life. She knew that was why she was born. She was well on her way to being the master of her destiny and a key resource person for her village and the surrounding communities.

Celestine kept very busy tending her plants and preparing medicinal remedies for the people who sent her prescription orders with her very capable helper, Leon, the same young man who had worked for Mama Atiwono. She also spent much time learning how to talk to the trees. As each tree species spoke with a different dialect, learning their languages was a real challenge and required hard work. Celestine proved to be one of the rare persons on Earth who was capable of achieving that daunting challenge.

The most important goal for Celestine was to learn how to talk to the baobab trees, but there were not any of those unusual trees growing near her forest enclave. She was strongly motivated to converse with the baobabs so she could see if there was a way to bring back Bobo, the father of her child. She was in a hurry because her belly was growing in size and there was little time left before she would give birth. She needed to find a way to leave her encampment to visit the nearest baobab tree, located several miles away in the dry savannah plain. That would be difficult to do, as she could not be seen outside her botanical domain.

The only way she could go to the baobab was to travel alone at night when the moon was full. She carefully calculated the paths she would take to go quickly and be unseen in the middle of the night to meet the baobab. She prayed to Mama Atiwono and all the grandfathers to guide and protect her from the mischievous spirits and dangerous snakes that would be lurking in the dark shadows of the night. She prayed to all the gods for the courage and strength needed to make the risky nocturnal foray.

In a loud and pleading voice she begged, "Almighty supreme God and all lesser gods and spirits, and all my grandfathers in the other world, I ask you to give me the courage I need and provide me with your protection. Bobo, I know you hear my prayers and you know what my heart seeks. I ask you to intervene as much as you can with the other spirits so that my journey will enjoy success. Amen."

The day came for Celestine to go to where the nearest baobab grew. She explained to the surrounding plants and trees surrounding why she had to go and asked them to pass the word on so that the baobab would be expecting her. She was careful not to make any sign that would reveal her plans to Leon. When the night had firmly grasped the Earth and the full moon shone like a giant beacon in the starlit sky, Celestine darted out of her compound like a scared lizard. She walked at a brisk pace, determined that nothing could stop her from seeing the baobab.

After two hours of walking without any let up, she spied in the moonlight the top branches of the magnificent baobab. That sight emboldened her. She marched firmly forward to within an arm's length of the baobab and began babbling in all the tree dialects she had learned, calling on the baobab to listen and respond. Her frantic pleas were met with only silence. She repeated her appeal for the baobab to talk to her until she was exhausted and could not say another word. She fell prostrate to the ground. Her clothes were soaked from heavy perspiration flowing from every pore. Not a sound could be heard. She felt her efforts had been futile and she was overcome by a sense of total hopelessness.

Celestine lifted her head and called again, "Please all gods, spirits, and grandfathers give me the additional strength I need to complete my mission. I will do anything to serve you if only you can help me do what I must do now. I beg you. Please, in the name of all that is good and right."

The moon was moving away, telling her she had to prepare to leave in order to return to her domain by sunrise. She struggled to lift herself up to begin the return leg of her perilous journey through the dark bush. When she turned around to start walking back, she heard a deep-throated chuckle. She halted in her tracks, turned toward the baobab, and listened intently. There were more chuckles, and then some words followed in a tree dialect she knew, but the words were difficult to understand because they were spoken in a heavy accent. She interpreted the words as saying, "You are weak. I know why you have come, but I cannot help you. Only the ancient baobab that swallowed Bobo can help you. Only this father of us all can tell you if Bobo can be brought back."

The words stopped and all became deathly silent again. Celestine had no time to think. She had to be on her way to avoid being seen so far from her domain in daylight. She forced herself to move quickly along the same paths as quietly as she had come. Morning was breaking as she entered her compound. The plants and trees were relieved to hear she was back and bombarded her with many questions about her trip. She felt drained and in no mood for any talk. She said in a firm voice, "You will have to wait. I need rest and some time to think. I will tell you all later."

It was hard for Celestine to rest or do anything. She was totally preoccupied by how she would visit the ancient baobab. She did not even know where that baobab was located and it was too far away to go there in one night. The only possibility she could think of was to enlist the support of her mother. She knew that involving her mother would bring her father into the act, as her mother could not do anything without telling her father. At that point, Celestine was so desperate she did not care what her father or anyone thought. She instructed Leon, "Tell my mother to come and visit me early tomorrow morning."

The first rays of sunlight were trickling through the trees when Celestine's mother, Evelyne, arrived. She was known for her pure heart and the decency she accorded every one she met. She was a simple, traditional woman who was happy with her station in life. Nobody had ever heard her complain. Everybody liked and respected Evelyne. Celestine was very close to her mother and their love for one another knew no boundaries. There was no doubt in Celestine's mind that she could count fully on her mother's cooperation.

Celestine told her mother in rapid nonstop sentences why it was absolutely necessary for her to go see the ancient baobab. Before she could ask her mother for assistance, her mom interrupted and told her, "I understand. I am ready to accompany you to see the old baobab anytime you want."

The calm and loving manner in which her mother said those words soothed Celestine, who no longer knew what to say. She did softly ask, "Where is this ancient baobab tree located?"

Her mother replied in the same serene voice, "This baobab is located at the far side of the wide stretch of savannah land west of the village. It is about a four-hour walk from here. We need to take food and water with us and plan to stay overnight at the foot of the baobab. We must also take a large plate of yam fufu as an offering to this oldest of all baobabs."

After a pause of a couple of minutes, Evelyne went on to gently note, "As you know, I must tell your father, but I will ask him to keep it our secret. We will leave early one morning and return on the afternoon of the next day. Have your helper, Leon, stay here for one night. Tell him you have an exceptional family emergency and you have to stay one night with me. My dear daughter, please be strong. This is a very good and right thing you are doing."

With her mother's every word, Celestine felt at peace and better prepared to do what she must do. All she could say was, "Mom, when can we go?"

Her mother smiled and quietly laughed as she said, "The day after tomorrow. I need a little time to prepare. Please do not worry so much, my beautiful daughter. I am so proud of what you have become."

Celestine, with tears in her eyes, gave her mom a big hug, and whispered, "At what time should I arrive at your house?"

Her mother replied, "Arrive at the same time I came here this morning, but do not come to the house. Nobody in the village should see you. I will meet you on the path that passes near the old iroko tree stump where you played as a child. I must go now before your father worries about my absence. I love you, my daughter. See you early in the morning of the day after tomorrow. Good bye now."

As Celestine watched her mom slowly walk down the path that led out of her compound, she felt encouraged and looked forward to confronting the old baobab with all her might and intelligence. She kept running through her mind what she would tell the old baobab and what tree dialects she would use. The old baobab must know that her pregnancy left her with no other choice but to have Bobo returned so he could confirm that he was indeed the father of the boy child growing in her womb. Most of all, she needed the world to know Bobo was the father of her child. She also loved and missed Bobo and wanted him to be her husband.

The next forty-eight hours passed in a speeding blur. Celestine hardly had enough time to catch up with all her chores, give instructions to Leon, and explain to the plants and trees why she would be gone for so long. While it was still dark on the morning of the appointed day, Celestine strapped onto her feet her best walking sandals and set off to meet her mom at the old stump of a giant iroko tree. Her mother was there waiting for her when she arrived. Celestine took some of the bundles her mom was carrying and placed the biggest one on her head and carried another at her side. She followed her mom step-by-step down the narrow path leading toward the tall savannah grassland.

Celestine and her mother walked quietly so nobody would hear them. After a couple hours, when the hot sun was burning their backs, they stopped to rest under a fan palm tree. They drank some water from a gourd Evelyne was carrying and ate a couple of handfuls of cassava flour mixed with peanuts. They wanted to tarry longer, but they knew they needed to press on so they could arrive at the ancient baobab while much daylight still remained. Silently they strode toward the baobab and the answers it hopefully had for Celestine.

Their excitement rose when they spied in the distance the topmost branches of the giant old baobab rising majestically over the savannah plain. That glorious sight helped quicken their pace. Celestine was feeling afraid, as she had never been in that place before. The old baobab was much larger than any tree she had ever seen. When they were about fifty yards from the baobab, they stopped to survey everything around them and take full stock of the magnificent baobab tree that towered before them. They felt puny and weak as they prepared to make their plea to the old baobab. For a moment, Celestine thought about forgetting the whole matter and turning about-face and going back to her secluded forest retreat.

Evelyne started to sing a chant in praise of the old baobab as she began walking toward it. Celestine followed her mother's cue and tried to sing the same short chant her mother was repeating. The words of that solemn tune went something like, "Almighty and forever wise baobab, we praise you and ask for your blessing."

They chanted those words until reaching the base of the baobab. They weaved their way through the many offering bowls left behind by other worshipers. When their faces were within inches of the tree, they knelt and prayed silently. Evelyne placed the big plate of yam fufu next to the tree and said, "Father of all baobab trees, we show our respect and honor you with this food. May we merit your blessing now and forever."

After that brief prayer, they rose and Celestine followed her mother as she walked around the wide trunk of the baobab five times while continuing to sing its praises. When they had finished their rounds, they returned to the spot where they had left the offering. Evelyne placed her hands on the tree. She whispered to

Celestine to do the same. "It is only by laying your hands on this tree that he can know you and what is in your heart," she said.

They both kept their hands on the tree for over ten minutes, and then Evelyne said, "There is nothing more for us to do. Let us sit down and wait to see if the baobab will send us a sign. This is the time you can start trying your tree talk with the baobab. Do not be afraid. Say why you are here and what you want."

Celestine found she was all choked up; it was difficult for her to think and talk. After clearing her throat many times, she laid her right hand on the baobab, introduced herself in a mixture of tree dialects, and explained why she had come so far. The more she talked, the more her courage increased. She raised the tone and intensity of her words. She was feeling very close to Bobo. Not far from her was the marble plaque that had been erected in his honor. That was the last place the earthly Bobo had been seen and she felt his presence near her. The feeling made her stress emphatically, "Master Baobab, I know Bobo is here. Please give him back to me and his child who grows daily in my stomach!" Her words were met by the silence that enveloped that remote corner of the open savannah.

It was late afternoon and the day was quickly drawing to a close. Celestine and her mom began to prepare to spend the night next to the baobab while beseeching its indulgence and intervention in returning Bobo. Evelyne thought aloud, "I think our chances of hearing anything from the baobab are better at night, particularly during the hour of the spirits around two in the morning."

Celestine and her mother prepared a place on the ground to lie down. They munched on cassava flour and peanuts. They tried to stay awake, but they eventually succumbed to sleep late in the night. Shortly after they fell asleep, a slight earth tremor woke them. Celestine was startled by what she began to hear and quickly sat straight-up, pointing to her ears to indicate to her mother that she was hearing something. Her mother's gaze was riveted on her daughter and the agitated way she was acting. For the first time, Evelyne was frightened.

Celestine stood up and got close to the baobab with her hands cupped over her ears. The voice she heard was rough, but the meaning it transmitted was clear. The old baobab told her in a few, almost unintelligible words, "I know why you have come. It is not possible for Bobo to return. His physical body has already been taken away. His ethereal spirit form is here and I can make his spirit appear to you and your mother. Do you want me to do this?"

Celestine was deeply disappointed that Bobo could not be returned in human form, but she was happy that his spirit could be revealed to her. Celestine quickly told her mom what was happening and then yelled at the top of her voice, "Show me Bobo's spirit."

Almost immediately after saying those words, a flickering gaseous replica of Bobo appeared. They stood speechless and in awe of the phantom that swayed back and forth as if blowing in the wind. Celestine struggled to compose herself and hold back her tears to say, "My darling, Bobo, can you not see your son growing in my stomach? Can't you say that you are indeed the father of the infant in my womb? Please, I beg you! Say what I ask!"

Bobo's smoky spirit moved toward Celestine and touched her stomach. At that enchanting moment, a clear voice came from the wavering image, "Celestine, I am sorry that I left you. Please take good care of our son. I will always be with you."

At that moment, the spirit evaporated and sounds of the night encroached again on the place of the master baobab. Celestine was in a state of shock and stood motionless. Her mother was afraid to make any movement. After a number of minutes, Celestine turned to her mom and asked, "Did you hear Bobo's spirit speak?

"Yes, my dear child, I heard every word and I will make sure your father knows that Bobo has recognized your child as his son."

There was nothing more they could do except thank the baobab and begin heading to their homes. The return walk was slow as they both were preoccupied by their nocturnal séance with the old baobab and the unworldly encounter with Bobo's spirit. Their feet felt heavy and they were uncertain of what to do next. They only wanted to go to their homes to rest and reflect deeply on what had happened in the light of the moon under the old baobab tree.

Evelyne knew she would have to tell her husband everything and he would seek the advice of his chiefly counterpart in Ataku on how to handle the birth of Bobo's son. There was no way they could keep that event secret, although it might be best for the villages if the paternity of Celestine's son remained a secret. It was an instance where the absence of transparency might be in the best interest of the two villages.

CHAPTER TEN
MORE MONEY, LESS POVERTY

The progress achieved brought both happiness and unhappiness to the people of Ataku and Aniko. They were delighted because their lives were better and very proud of their achievements. They were also happy with all the outsiders who visited their villages and praised their good works. But, that happiness only worked to raise their expectations. The more they achieved, the more they could see how much more they needed to do. Before, they were resigned to their poverty, but their eyes had been opened and they resented what they did not have. In the past they were able to live with their "glass" being half-full, but they could no longer abide with it being half-empty.

They had achieved much, but they had not yet done anything to improve what their livelihoods depended on the most: agriculture. The vast majority of the villagers practiced subsistence agriculture, hoping to produce enough food to carry them from one annual harvest to another. Any household monetary income generated depended mainly on one cash crop: cacao. Every family had some cacao, and the sale of the beans from their cacao trees was the main source of income. The only way to increase their income was to increase the production of cacao, but doing so was fraught with a number of formidable obstacles.

The yields of existing cacao trees were low because they were old and disease-ridden. The soil had been depleted by many years of constant cultivation. The cacao crop required the shade of big indigenous trees, but so many of those trees had been cut down over the years that shade had become insufficient. The international market price for cacao beans was so low that it was hardly worth the labor involved with harvesting and processing the beans for sale to local representatives of the companies that exported the crop. People had to produce twice the beans that they did five years ago to earn the money needed to buy the same things. Twenty years ago a single family could manage well a couple acres of cacao, and with the money generated from the sale of the annual harvest they could buy a low-priced car. Today, the same amount of production could not buy a car tire.

In the face of a lower crop price and declining yields, what could the people do to increase the income they derived from agriculture? There were not any other cash crops suitable to the local climatic and soil conditions. They had tried cultivating cotton, but that effort ended in utter failure as the climate was not suited for growing that crop. There were not any viable options to improving the yields of their cacao fields. They needed to obtain higher-yielding varieties that were also disease resistant. That would not be easy. The demand for those new varieties outstripped the supply available at government agricultural research stations. Somehow they needed to acquire a few dozen seedlings of the improved varieties and reproduce them in their own nurseries.

It was obvious to the people that the matter was larger than any single individual's ability to address. They would therefore have to band together if they were to be successful in improving cacao production. A few of the more successful farmers created an association. They invited all other cacao farmers to join them. As too many people turned up for their first meeting, they decided to limit representation to one person per household. The women complained about that decision, as they feared all the representatives would be men. The complaint prompted a decision that allowed women to form their own association and name representatives to participate on the governing council of the main association. The women insisted on having thirty percent of the seats on the governing council. The men reluctantly agreed to that condition. Involving the women in that manner was quite a profound change, as women had not previously participated along with men in any such groups.

The first meeting of the Ataku-Aniko Cacao Growers Association (abbreviated as AACG, or simply referred to as 'AA') was devoted to electing officers and establishing a working agenda. It was decided the president of the association should be the man with the largest farm and the vice president should be a small farmer from another family. Generally the larger cacao fields were near Ataku. Care was taken so that each village was fairly represented. It was also decided that the secretary and treasurer should be literate women. People quickly put forth those candidates they could trust to do a good job and represent their best interests. Votes were taken by raising hands. Everyone was in a very enthusiastic and cooperative mood. They were primed to achieve great things together.

A committee was named to investigate how to obtain seedlings of resistant varieties. They knew the only place to obtain those seedlings was at the government research station located about thirty miles away. At that point, the only people receiving those varieties were top members of the president's political party and his corrupt cronies. The station was run like the president's private farm. In the past, there were times when seedlings could be bought on the black market, but lately the president had cracked harshly down on such crooked schemes.

The only known way for the villages to obtain seedlings would be to steal them. That was a very high-risk undertaking, but it was better than continuing to suffer from stagnating crop yields. A small group was selected to study in secret how to steal seedlings from the station without being caught. From the onset, they decided not to involve the chiefs. They were better off not knowing about the criminal activity. Of course, nothing could happen in the villages without the chiefs knowing, but enough distance had to be maintained from the chiefs so they could deny having any knowledge of the risky venture.

Committee members agreed the risks were high, but if they could steal fifty or so seedlings without being caught, the gains would be huge for their villages. For all those concerned, the risk was well worth it. They were convinced all they needed to do was to plan and time the theft of seedlings carefully. Ten people were asked to volunteer for the perilous mission. They all had to be physically fit so they could walk the long distance to and from the station. The return trip would be even more perilous, as they would have to strap a bag with five or more seedlings to their back. The round trip journey could take up to three days on foot.

A group of ten held a secret nighttime planning session. After lengthy and sometimes heated exchanges, the designated leader of the group, Gerson, summed up their plan by saying. "We will move on a moonless night when we are sure it will rain. We will dress in black and cover our bodies with dark mud. We will walk barefoot and avoid making any sound. All communications will be by hand gestures. We cannot make any noise!"

They met several times to go over every detail of their plan. They would walk to a secluded place within five miles of the station and wait until it was raining hard to go to the station. They knew the station guards would take refuge in their small shelters if it were raining. Using the cover of rain at night to rob the seedlings was essential to the success of their plan. When they were certain no guard was around, the slimmest person in the group would crawl under the sturdy chain-link fence and rapidly gather and carefully hand seedlings in their plastic pots to others waiting just outside the fence. In reality, security at the station was poor because nobody could imagine that anyone would dare steal from the president. As soon as one person had a full load of seedlings, he would start walking back to a designated place in the forest located several miles away and wait for the others to arrive.

A dark, rainy night arrived and all were in position to go to the station and steal seedlings. Everyone was very nervous and afraid, but for the good of their communities they upped their courage and boldly headed on their way as planned. They trudged along back paths that had not been used for years. They knew it would not take long for each person to load his quota of seedlings on his back and move swiftly to the rendezvous point in spite of the downpour. They would be soaked to the bone, but all that mattered was making it possible for their villages to have a better future. If need be, they were prepared to sacrifice their lives to achieve their mission.

Some people did not approve of such risk taking. They could not accept that such high risks would be taken in spite of the fact it might be ten years before any benefits from the new seedlings would be reaped. Most people lived on the edge of survival and they had never planned ahead much. Their interests were in satisfying their needs in the present since there might not be any tomorrow. There was a local saying: "My needs today are more important than my life." They did not want to hear about what could be done for them in the future. The only thing they wanted to hear was how you could help them today. They had survived for generations by living for the day. Planning ahead was an alien concept. The usual modus operandi was to work to buy time.

Everyone, even those who disagreed, were happy to learn that "operation seedlings" had been a success and all the seedlings were alive and well in a hidden place in the forest. That place had been prepared well beforehand. It was an ideal spot, as it was difficult to find, had a water spring, and ample shade. Only those who carried the seedlings knew of the secluded location of the clandestine nursery. In particular, no information about the operation was revealed to the chiefs in order to protect them. If the government authorities discovered any involvement of the chiefs with the operation, the consequences for them and the villages would be quite severe.

Things would be bad enough for those involved if they were caught and found guilty. For the villagers, stealing from the government was not like stealing from a person, which was very bad. The only bad thing would be if you were caught stealing from the government. Getting caught meant you were a failure and had not planned well your crime against the government. Anyone dumb enough to be caught for stealing from the government deserved the harsh punishment that would surely be meted out to him or her. Such thieves were not given any pity. People thought getting caught by the government was a most unforgivable crime. Anyway, no one thought that the number of seedlings stolen would be noticed, as the research station contained thousands of cacao plants.

A difficult challenge facing the AACG Association was how to determine the distribution of the one hundred seedlings that had been stolen in the best interest of the community. Association members had long and heated discussions on that almost irresolvable subject. After many meetings, the association president, Ernest, announced, "It has been decided that those with the oldest trees will receive the new seedlings. We believe this is a good decision, as these people are usually the ones whose families began farming cacao first. Also, the location of most of these farmers in one geographical area facilitates distribution."

There were, however, serious drawbacks to being among the first to receive the new and improved tree varieties. All their old trees would have to be dug up, chopped into pieces, and burnt. That was the only way disease from those old trees could be prevented from spreading. In that respect, it was also good that the oldest farms were mostly located in one area.

The initial beneficiaries were worried about how they would survive during the years it would take the new seedlings to mature. They also worried about all the extra labor involved with destroying their old trees. And, other food crops would not grow well in the shaded areas used for cacao. The association discussed those weighty matters at length. It was decided by a majority vote that other members of the association who could still benefit from cacao production should contribute to the support of those who would take the risk of pioneering the cultivation of new varieties. After all, everyone else would depend on the good work of those pioneer farmers to produce more seedlings from the initial trees for wider distribution. Everyone had a stake in that first pilot effort from which it would take years to reap any benefits. The risks were high, but the potential gain was also high. Failure would mean the end of the primary livelihood and source of income for the villages. It was either suffer more poverty or try to renew their cacao fields.

Another important catch to the introduction of the new varieties was the required application of fertilizer to produce high yields. That requirement obliged the AACG to set up a committee for the acquisition and application of imported chemical fertilizer. Few people used that key commodity. It was too expensive and difficult to obtain. The few people in the villages who used the vital input only did so in very small amounts. To increase cacao production, relatively large amounts of fertilizer would be needed. Nobody knew how to acquire appreciable quantities of the right type of that scarce input. If they did acquire the several tons of fertilizer needed, how would they pay for its transport and storage? There remained many important but unanswered questions.

The level of sophistication required to deal with those issues was beyond the competency of the association. It was clear they would need external assistance to calculate the amount of fertilizer they should apply, and when and how it should be applied. They really needed help in elaborating a business plan. The problem was how to find such help. After much discussion, people hung their heads in defeat. There appeared to be no way to avoid failure and doomed futures. Who could come to their aid?

One man in their group could not contain his anxiety and called loudly out, "Is there no one in the entire country who can help us?"

From the back row of their meeting place under a straw-covered hangar, a hardly audible voice said, "I know where we can find help." All heads turned to see from where those softly spoken words came. They all spied a timid teenage boy dressed in his old khaki school uniform who had been observing from a distance the frustrated proceedings. Normally people of his age were not involved in such deliberations and were expected to remain aloof and quiet.

The president of the association demanded, "Stand up, identify yourself, and speak loudly so all can hear."

The young man slowly stood up. He was so scared that it took him time to say anything. He finally screwed up his courage and quickly said, "My older brother went to work in cacao plantations in a neighboring country after finishing his primary schooling here." After blurting out those words, he quickly fell into his seat.

Immediately the young man was bombarded with questions. Everyone was asking him about the same thing at the same time. The association president yelled at the top of his voice, "Every one, please be quiet and seated! Please speak one at a time!"

Once order and calm were restored to the meeting, the president gently called, "Young man, please do not be afraid. Come join me in the front. We need to listen carefully to what you have to say about your brother's capacity to help us."

The young man did as asked and marched briskly to the front bench and stood next to the president. The president stared at the young man, smiled and then he said, "Talk loudly. We need some good news!"

The young man was very dark in complexion and short for his age. Many people in the meeting had a difficult time seeing him. To the surprise of all, when he began talking it was in a booming, authoritative voice. "I, Germain, can firmly state that my older brother, Gregoire, has had good experience in all things related to cacao growing and processing. He has worked for two years in big commercial plantations where he had the opportunity to learn everything. He is coming home for his vacation tomorrow, so you can talk to him yourself."

Before Germain could finish his words, a huge wave of collective relief washed over all present. Everybody's spirits had reversed their downward trend, and they were now running high. People were already seeing Gregoire as their savior. They could not wait to meet Gregoire and see how he could help them get their cacao production back on track and keep it on track. There was nothing more to do but wait for Gregoire's arrival.

The days passed and Gregoire did not arrive. The people were worried that he would not arrive in time to allow them to prepare for the next agricultural season and, consequently, they would have to wait another year until the onset of the following rainy season. The thought of losing another year after they had dared to steal new cacao seedlings was almost too much to bear. Just when they were about to give up hope of Gregoire arriving in time to avoid the loss of the year, the local grapevine broadcast the exciting news of his arrival. Old men who still knew the language of the talking drums beat loudly the exciting news on the old leather-topped iroko tom-toms and sounded high praises for Gregoire. People could not wait to have a session with Gregoire. Association leaders rushed to confirm a meeting with him just before sundown on the very day of his much welcomed arrival.

Gregoire was confused by the unexpected warm welcome accorded him by the villages. He had come home for a quiet visit of a couple weeks with his family, and he planned to return to his job in the cacao fields of a large commercial farm in a neighboring country. He did not know what to think about all the excitement his arrival had generated. He was treated like royalty and did not know what he had done to deserve such a grand reception.

Association leaders went to Gregoire's family compound to accompany him to the meeting site. While they walked, they briefed Gregoire about why they were interested in him. Gregoire could see that they were after his knowledge of cacao farming. He became more relaxed when that was made clear to him because it was a subject he really knew something about. By the time they arrived at the meeting venue, Gregoire was standing proud and content because he believed he did have something to offer to the villages.

The president of the association asked everyone to take their places and be quiet. He asked Gregoire to stand beside him. He introduced him to all present and explained why Gregoire was important to achieving the association's goal of increasing cacao production. Gregoire was enjoying the moment and could not wait to reveal how much he knew about cacao cultivation and processing. Gregoire looked very different from his younger brother Germain. He was tall, well-groomed, and wore wire-rimmed spectacles. He dressed like a businessman and not like a farmer. He carried in his breast pocket a pen and a small notebook and wore an expensive wristwatch. Even before he opened his mouth, the people could see he was a person they should take seriously.

One thing Gregoire had in common with his brother was a loud, booming voice that was easy to hear and comprehend. Everyone was all ears when Gregoire began rattling off in a very professional manner many facts and figures about cacao. He began by asserting, "Modern cacao growing is not hard to do if you have all the inputs, and do the work in the right way. Old trees must be destroyed by burning and new trees planted at the correct depth and prescribed spacing. The best fertilizer type for your soils must be applied around the tree at the proper distance and depth. Each tree must be carefully tended and pruned in the right manner. The proper amount of shade must be provided. Mature cacao pods must be cut and handled in the right manner. Cacao beans must be processed in the right way to fetch the best price. If all these things are to be done in the correct way, you need the "right" person to manage the business of cacao production. To be successful, you can no longer be simple farmers. You must be businessmen and this entails that each of you have a business plan for your cacao farm."

When Gregoire had finished speaking, there was not the loud applause he expected. There was so much silence you could hear a pin drop. The people were not upset with what he said, but perplexed by the new concepts he had introduced. Their ignorance of much of what he said left them speechless. Their main impression was they were lost without someone like Gregoire to help them. They could see they had to learn all Gregoire knew or they would be condemned to remaining subsistence farmers, stuck in a downward spiral of poverty. When they did begin mumbling to each other, it was all about how they must make it so Gregoire would remain with them and share all he knew about cacao farming.

After a long pause, the president stood and called the session to order. He cleared his voice and spoke in an uncertain manner, "We thank you, Mr. Gregoire, for that eye-opening presentation. We are very impressed by your obvious competency in cacao farming, or as you say, cacao business. I think we can easily see we still have much to learn about cultivating cacao in the modern way, as we must do if we are to achieve our objectives. We find ourselves in the awkward position of pleading with you to remain here and help us. We appeal to your sense of allegiance to your community. We believe you must give top priority to your home people."

Gregoire remained calm and expressionless, but deep down he really did want to stay home and help his people. His problem was he could not help for free. He stood up and smiled, "I am very touched by your request for my help. I would be pleased to stay here, but I also need to make money for my family. Is there no way for you to pay me something as the technical manager of your association? You have much to do to become a viable cacao production association. You need bylaws and rules that govern the association and its membership, making it eligible for receiving at discounted prices necessary inputs. I will spare you all the details now but, trust me, you have much to do to become a modern association of cacao producers."

Again, Gregoire's words had the people's heads spinning and searching for a way to keep Gregoire home. The president announced a brief recess to give him time to talk with other leaders. The recess lasted longer than expected, but when it ended, the president was able to announce, "We are prepared to take up a monthly collection among our membership to pay Gregoire a salary for managing our association and providing us with the technical know-how we need to achieve higher cacao yields and sales. We will also compensate Gregoire by providing him a cacao field to cultivate. This field will also serve as a demonstration plot to teach all of us how to improve cacao production. We are pleased to say that Gregoire has graciously accepted our employment proposal. I will take him with us tomorrow when we inform our chiefs of the good news."

The people left the meeting singing, thanking God, and shouting the praises of Gregoire. Before leaving, each one went up to Gregoire to shake his hand and pat him on the back. There was much laughter. The people were happy again. Gregoire's agreement to stay with them had raised their hopes and made them believe a better future was possible. They were convinced that with Gregoire's expert help, hard work, and perseverance they could improve their lives and lay the foundation for a better future for their children and grandchildren. At the insistence of the grandfathers, it was firmly embedded in their oral history that the success or failure of each succeeding generation would be judged on whether or not it had left behind a better world for those who followed them.

CHAPTER ELEVEN
OUTSIDE INTERFERENCE

Chiefs Yofu and Gyasi were happy to meet Gregoire and to hear the hopeful news about the revitalization of cacao, the mainstay of their local economy. They enjoyed their meeting with the AACG leaders and Gregoire. They managed to keep happy faces in spite of the deep anxiety a menacing telegram from a senior government official was causing them. The ominous telegram from the capital city of Melomti had arrived earlier in the day. As they had feared, the success of their villages had not gone unnoticed, and corrupt government officials wanted to weasel their way into the limelight and profits. It appeared their good deeds would not go unpunished.

The telegram briefly stated that the minister of interior would be coming to observe firsthand the success achieved by the two villages. The minister was the most dreaded man in the country. Hearing his name, Hamma, was enough to strike fear into the hearts of even the most courageous. He was the president's most trusted aide and the one sent to investigate any deviation from the prevailing authoritarian power structure. The president's policy was to have tight control over the entire country, especially where money was concerned. Any person or village wanting to venture outside the expected norm would need the agreement of the president, who would always insist on his cut. It was either the president's way or the highway, or often much worse.

Minister Hamma was a poorly educated man, but he had well-honed survival instincts, which helped make him the only remaining minister from the original group of senior officials who supported the president's military coup over thirty years ago. All the other ministers had disappeared in one of the president's secret gulags, or publicly executed on trumped up charges. Often those who fell out of favor were locked up by the president and left to die from the "black diet." That meant no water or food in an almost hermetically sealed cell. That inhuman death was often reserved for senior officials who became too popular. The same could happen to anyone who appeared to diminish the importance of the president, or shared too much in the high honors and glory that were reserved only for the president.

Minister Hamma had much blood on his hands and was considered to be the president's hatchet man. He was an exceptional person in many ways. He did not have any family and nobody knew where he came from. It was rumored that he had been abandoned as a baby and raised by the president. He had served in every ministerial post. The president was constantly trying to keep his ministers off balance by rotating them to different posts each year. The president once made a humorous, but revealing statement, to a visiting diplomat. He said, "I have three kinds of ministers: one that is actually a minister, one who is in jail, and one who is in exile, and I rotate them to one of these three slots each year."

The only exception to that rule was Minister Hamma who was also rumored to be the president's bastard son.

In his previous post as minister of finance, Hamma was known as Mister "Ten Percent." Any financial deal or anything involving money had to go through him before going to the president, and before he would consider any project, he had to be guaranteed a ten percent cut. In that position, he was also in control of the customs service and government buildings office. Those two entities were great repositories of money, and he made sure that he and the president got their share. Anywhere there was money they had to be part of the deal. It was rumored that Hamma kept large sums of money in metal trunks in his house in a room made of thick iron sheets. That room was always air-conditioned and watched around-the-clock by heavily armed guards.

There was a story people heard about Hamma and the high-level of corruption he managed. It was said that he once visited a minister of finance in an Asian country and was impressed by the way he was able to rake off large amounts of money. He went to the minister's luxurious villa, and the Asian minister laughingly pointed to the road they were driving on and said, "Ten percent." He went on to say that by pocketing 10 percent of the road's contract cost he was able to build his villa and send his children to boarding schools in Europe. That encounter gave Hamma new ideas about how he and the president could increase their already immense wealth.

Some years later, the Asian minister visited Hamma's country and was taken by the president to his ultra-expensive palace located in a remote mountain chain in the far north of the country. That palace was equipped with all the latest gadgets and sported gold-plated sink faucets and toilet handles. A top European decorator furnished it. The palace remained empty most of the time, except when the president wanted to show it off to important visitors.

He took the visiting Asian minister to his palace in his latest model helicopter. While flying at a low level to the palace, the president asked the minister if he could see the new highway below. The minister looked out both windows of the helicopter repeatedly, but he could not see any highway. A bit embarrassed, he finally admitted, "Mr. President. I am sorry, but I do not see any highway."

The president chuckled and smiled when he said, "One hundred percent."

With that simple and clear answer, the president was trying to impress upon his Asian visitor that he was so all-powerful he could take all the funds that had been budgeted for the highway. He did not know that when he said that, the Asian minister saw him to be a fool. After all, anyone knew that you could not take everything if the country was to grow and prosper. The Asian minister knew you had to be very careful to limit corruption so the country could achieve its economic and social goals. Some greed was understandable, but total greed was wrong and counterproductive.

The chiefs suffered terrible bouts of anguish. They knew that the powerful Hamma always got his way. If they attempted to defy his wishes, the consequences would be quite harsh. They knew the main thing that attracted him to their villages was the scent of money and the president's intense dislike for anything positive happening in his country for which he was not given credit.

The chiefs spent long hours together trying to elaborate a successful strategy for dealing with Hamma when he arrived in their villages the next week. They planned a huge feast accompanied by dancers, drummers, and singers to honor and flatter Hamma. They would make him a gift of an expensive traditional gown with vibrant embroidered designs. They would treat him like a king and cater to his every whim.

All their foreign friends would be invited to the festive reception for Hamma. That invitation of white people was something of a protective measure. Hamma would be reluctant to do anything bad in front of outsiders. Families with young and beautiful daughters were instructed to keep them inside their houses. It was widely known that Hamma also scouted for new wives for the president. If he saw a young woman he thought the president would like, she would be forced to go to the capital city and join the president, who had many wives and dozens of children. The president's secret plan was to have at least one child with a woman from each district in the country. He believed in that way he could more tightly control the entire country and ensure his offspring would rule after his death. He called that reproduction strategy the "permanent solution."

The biggest challenge facing the chiefs was how to find a way to keep Hamma's hands off the additional revenue the villages were generating from their various new activities. They were prepared to accord the president all the glory for their achievements, but they wanted to preserve their growing funding stream to support needed projects in their communities. They saw the best way to do that was to downplay the amount of income they were receiving from visitors and the modest road toll. They thought that amount of money would be of no interest to the multimillionaire president who owned large tracts of land, many villas in every town, and properties in Europe. Surely their measly community projects fund would represent nothing to him.

Every clan and family head were told to be very careful regarding anything they said to Hamma or anyone accompanying him. It was stressed that villagers were not to mention anything about cacao. They were told to act happy and to say that, in spite of some improvements, they were still struggling with their poverty.

As usual, there was too little money and too much hunger. They wanted Hamma to see that it was just another poor village full of ignorant and miserable people in need of any assistance he could provide them. They hoped that he would see them as too poor to abuse, or ask for anything.

The dreaded day arrived for Hamma's visit. People stood along the road from the main highway to the villages waving palm branches. When Hamma approached, they sang songs of praise for him and the president. Hamma arrived in a brand new black Toyota Land Cruiser with a sliding roof opening that allowed him to stand up and wave at the people welcoming him. His vehicle was followed by a military pickup full of well-armed soldiers. Next to him in his vehicle were two armed guards dressed in black suits and ties, and wearing dark sunglasses. It was hard for the people to sing happy songs in the face of such a menacing sight.

Hamma was escorted to the nicely decorated podium that had been set up at some expense in the public place in Ataku. A huge photo of the president was displayed in an elevated position behind the podium. Village carpenters had taken care to build the podium so it would be lower than the short but burly Hamma. Following the impressive presentations of drumming, dancing, and acrobatic groups, Chief Yofu took the stand to solemnly introduce Hamma. He raised his arms so that people would know to be absolutely quiet. In a loud and firm voice that was uncharacteristic of him, Chief Yofu exclaimed, "We have the great honor today to have among us one of the country's most accomplished children, Minister Hamma." Loud and prolonged applause and noisemaking resounded to denote the joy people had for being chosen for the visit by one of the country's highest dignitaries.

The short and fat, high and mighty Hamma strutted toward the podium, noting his appreciation of the accolades showered on him by waving his ornamental fly whisk up and down in all directions. He tightly held the red goat leather whisk handle as he made its foot-long white cow hair strands dance in slow motion. He was dressed in the latest European fashion, wearing a double-breasted dark blue suit and an expensive designer's tie. He wore a handmade dress shirt with very visible golden cuff links. The suit was well tailored, but nothing could really fit his obtuse body well. His legs were too short and his stomach popped out like a basketball. He looked very awkward and uncomfortable. His suit jacket was fully and tightly buttoned. It appeared as if the buttons could give way at any moment under the constant strain caused by his protruding potbelly.

Hamma walked to the podium in a wobbly gait as he wore elevator shoes to appear taller. The huge ego of that very paranoid man largely compensated for his physical shortcomings. He knew he could inflate himself with self-importance and lord it over all because of his close links to the president. Without those links, he would be a disrespected nobody, unsuited for any position in society. The people worked hard to keep smiling and mask their real feelings for that unworthy individual. Everyone worked together to make Hamma believe the opposite of what was true. They pretended in the most convincing way possible that Hamma was well respected and admired.

Before he said any words, Hamma smiled at everyone as if wanting to show off his protruding, oversized, and very white teeth. To the people he looked like an ape ready to jump on their small children and devour them. He was really a scary sight, and it took much effort and courage for the people to smile back at him and treat him like royalty. A full beard accentuated his very dark complexion. He had a wide nose that pushed flat up against his head, giving him a pig-like appearance. He was constantly wiping the sweat pouring off his protruding brow with a large white handkerchief.

In his high-pitched, squeaky voice he preached, "My dear fellow citizens, thank you for your very warm welcome. I am very happy to be here among you today to represent our beloved national guide and president. The president has heard favorable reports on your many accomplishments, and he has sent me to see firsthand what you have achieved. Today I will be meeting with your leaders to learn more about your activities so I can report back to the president. Thank you for your understanding. Now, please let me lead you in a new song of praise created by his most high excellency, our President Nasungu."

People were having a hard time suppressing their laughter over how funny Hamma looked and sounded. He was the most ridiculous person they had ever seen. It was almost too much when he tried to lead them in a dim-witted song that used the music from a well-known and much loved traditional song. They strained to understand and follow the nonsensical words filtering through Hamma's screechy voice. They thought the whimsical ditty went something like,

"Why go to Paris? Why go to London? Why go anywhere when you have such nice lives in a beautiful country?

You have your liberty and freedom in an independent and progressive country! Why go where you are not wanted and will not have any of these rights?

Stay home and enjoy life more than you can anywhere else. Don't go and be a stranger somewhere else.

Stay home and work to make your country strong and happy."

It was hard for the people to sing those stupid words with Minister "Ten Percent," but they had no choice but to make a good show of it. They knew the latest idiotic propaganda jingo promoted by the government was aimed at discouraging people from leaving the country. A large part of the country's population had voted with its feet and left the country to escape the oppressive vagaries of the protracted dictatorship. In particular, young men had left in great numbers, leaving some villages without enough men to do agricultural labor. The regime resented that some of the people had formed opposition groups in the countries where they resided.

The negative, but usually truthful, reports published by those groups were galling to the government, which used heavy-handed methods to put a stop to them. That included threatening the families and villages of those associated with members of those groups. It also included sending spies to infiltrate those groups and capture their leaders so they could be brought home for harsh judgment. Anyone believed to be speaking out against the government would be severely beaten and tortured until they renounced their unacceptable views and told the "truth" the president wanted to hear. Once the government was satisfied it had reformed some of those individuals, they would have them speak on national radio, confessing to how wrong they were and how great the president was. That situation created two kinds of "truth": the real truth and the truth the president wanted to hear. Those who were not willing to produce the latter were left in their dark cells to die.

The president was particularly concerned about one group based in Europe that was becoming very strong and had gained the ear of European politicians and the international media. His anger with that group pushed him to take exceptional measures. He was prepared to take high risks to capture the leader of that group and bring him home to face his cruel justice. He sent an elite team from his presidential guard on his private jet to Europe, ordering them to find the leader and bring him back or they, and their families, would suffer a horrible fate. With that kind of fearful motivation, the team was imbued with the absolute need to

accomplish their mission. They knew very well what terrible consequences awaited them if they failed.

That highly committed team arrived in Europe and was able
to find and track the opposition group leader. Clandestinely, they
studied from a distance his every move and noted his usual routines. They observed that along the route he took home every evening there were a number of dead end alleys. Their plan was to
lure him into one of those alleys so they could drug him and use
their diplomatic passes to haul him in a crate to the president's
plane. They paid a sexy young woman to entice him into the dark
alley. Once he was in the alley they would enter and chase him to
the end of the alley where they would pounce on him and give him
an injection of a strong tranquilizer.

Their plan worked just as they had hoped. As soon as the
woman fled the alley entrance, they entered and chased the man
to the back of the alley. They had him cornered and were ready to
pounce on him when a very strange and unanticipated thing happened. The man evaporated and turned into a cloud of mist. From
that mist came a black cat that quickly climbed over the back wall
of the alley and sped away. The team was stunned and frightened
by what had happened. They had heard of people transforming
into animals, but they never thought they would see such a thing
themselves. There was no doubt that the opposition leader possessed powerful magic. That was a very scary fact, but not as scary
as what would happen to them when they reported back to the
president.

The team was completely silent as they took the long flight
home. Immediately after landing they were whisked off in a palace
vehicle to see the president in his well-guarded residence. They
were marched into the living room where the president was waiting for them. They were so full of fear their leader could not find

his voice until one of the president's special guards hit him on the back with his cowhide whip. The leader whelped like a small puppy, dropped to his knees, and cried, "Mr. President we beg you for your pardon. We were not able to bring home the evildoer."

Upon hearing those disappointing words, the president savagely slapped the leader across his head with his wood cane. The leader fell to the floor crying for mercy. The president bellowed, "Stop acting like a bunch of school girls! Quit your gibberish and tell me what happened. Tell me now before I hit you again!"

The leader sat up on the floor and bawled, "Mr. President, we had him in our grasp, but he turned into a black cat and ran away."

Those words made the president the most frightened man in the room. He quietly gave instructions to his guards to take the men out, beat them soundly for their failure, and then assign them to remote locations where nobody would listen to them. He needed time to think. He was quite shocked that the opposition leader possessed the power to transform himself into a black cat. That told him he was dealing with more than mere human forces. First thing the next morning he would assemble his group of high-powered fetish priests that he had gathered around him from all parts of the country and ask them for the magic he needed to combat those who could transform themselves into animals. If the opposition were going to resort to using occult powers, he would one-up them with his powerful group of fetish priests.

To the dour chagrin of all the people, Minister Hamma insisted on repeating his silly propaganda song three times. To the people, the repetition of the stupid song only made it harder to accept. The people were relieved when Hamma finally wished them farewell and toadied off to meet the chiefs and other community leaders. Before he left the podium, as was the custom, he was given many gifts by the people, including large baskets of fruits and yams, some chickens, and a few live goats. He signaled to the soldiers to come and collect the gifts and put them in their pickup. His body-guards accompanied him to Chief Yofu's compound where they could meet in the quiet of the chief's judgment house.

Hamma entered the narrow door to the house first, grating the sides of his corpulent body as he passed into the room. Chiefs Yofu and Gyasi quickly followed him. A special throne chair had been put in place for Hamma to occupy. The remainder of the people filed through the door and sat next to the chiefs on wooden benches. As soon as the last person was seated, Hamma rudely dispensed with all protocol, took charge of the meeting, and began telling his audience in a blunt, authoritative tone what was on his mind. The fact that he had refused the large calabash of freshly harvested palm wine handed to him by the chief's senior wife had everyone worried. That unusually impolite gesture certainly suggested he was a very uncultivated and cruel man.

Without looking at the men sitting before him, Hamma roughly growled, "I do not have time, so I will tell you what I have been sent to say. The president is upset because you are doing a lot of things without letting the government know and you are not acknowledging any support from the president. This has to stop! Also, you must stop your roadwork and collecting any tolls on the road leading to your villages. The government is responsible for this road, so stop doing anything on the road! I hope my words are clear because I do not want to come back."

After a lengthy pause, all Chiefs Yofu and Gyasi dared say was, "We have heard and we understand."

When Hamma heard that response, he abruptly stood up and said he had to go. He briskly exited the room with his two body-guards without saying good-bye. The chiefs struggled to keep up with him as he left the compound and entered his chauffeured luxury vehicle. His driver stepped on the accelerator and he drove off at a speed that had never been seen before in the village. He did not look back or wave. It was as if he was devoid of any human feelings and was completely divorced from the norms of the local society.

Hamma's awful behavior was hard for the chiefs and their entourage to stomach. They were angry and hurt by what Hamma had told them. All this was more difficult to accept because Hamma was considered a stranger without manners or education. They did not want to give the president any credit for what they could achieve themselves. Moreover, the loss of toll fees would deal an almost fatal blow to the community development fund. They were in a rebellious mood, but they knew that the president was watching them closely. The slightest misstep would result in soldiers being sent to commit unspeakable atrocities against them. Their hearts were crying. The progress they hungered for could not be achieved because of government interference. As long as the government had to be involved with their affairs, they were condemned to stay poor and unhappy. Hamma's short visit had shattered all their dreams and made it impossible for them to make a better future for themselves. They felt damned and helpless.

CHAPTER TWELVE
LUNAR ECLIPSE

Those were very troubling days for the villages of Ataku and Aniko. Chiefs Yofu and Gyasi were reluctant to inform their senior elders and clan heads about what Minister Hamma had told them. They found it hard to be the bearers of such bad news. They wished there was some alternative, but they had no choice. It was necessary and their duty to convey to the leaders of their villages the words told to them by Hamma. That burden weighed heavily on them. They knew Hamma's decision would wreck the progress their villages had achieved and plunge the villagers into a deep state of depression.

Village criers quietly disseminated the word to the senior leaders, telling them to come to a meeting at Chief Yofu's compound the next day just when the sun was rising above the summit of Mount Ataku. The unusual silent way the criers delivered the invitation was foreboding. They usually banged on their iron gong-gongs and yelled out their message at every thirty paces. Messages were only delivered silently when it was about the death of a chief or some prominent elder. That was, therefore, a portentous sign.

All those invited were worried in advance about the bad news they would receive.

From all parts of the villages, men slowly ambled along the foot trails that led to the chief's compound. Not a word was spoken among them. Everyone in the village could see them headed to the chief's compound in a somber mood. Their hearts sank, as they knew the news they would hear was not good. The men crowded into one of the chief's drab circular meeting houses that was in disrepair and in need of new roofing thatch. There were not enough benches for all of them to sit. They stood until the chiefs entered and sat on benches facing them. On the few remaining benches, the oldest elders were seated and the rest of the twenty or so men sat on the floor.

In the flickering light of early morning kerosene lanterns, Chief Yofu carefully studied the group, looking intently at each man, one by one, straight into their eyes. Chief Yofu's droopy face could not hide his deep anguish. He took a deep breath and opened the meeting by saying in a troubled soft voice, "Greetings to all. I have asked you to come here because my brother, Chief Gyasi, and I have some very bad news to tell you. As you know, Minister Hamma spoke to us. He ordered us to stop all roadwork and toll collections. He also told us that we have to give more credit to President Nasungu for everything we do."

Before he could continue, Chief Yofu was interrupted by the loud and rancorous reaction his words generated. Those in attendance were genuinely shocked and very upset by the bad news. All were very agitated and tried to speak at once. They repeated to one another that Hamma's instructions were very wrong. One man, Akan, known for his sharp tongue and assertive manners, stood up and raised his fist, saying, "Enough is enough, we cannot take it anymore! We will rebel no matter what!"

Normally, that outspoken man would have been ignored because his views were always too radical to accept. That time, however, there were some men in the group who were nodding their heads in agreement with him. Others clapped their hands to support what he was saying. The men were infuriated. The growing tension in the stuffy room was palpable.

The chiefs feared things were getting out of hand. Uncharacteristically, they raised their voices, demanding order and quiet. Once calm had been restored, Chief Gyasi took his turn to talk. He spoke in a more businesslike fashion, adding firmly, "Stop kidding yourselves! You know very well the consequences of disobeying the president. If we do not do as we have been told, he will for sure send his soldiers and some of us will be severely beaten, others will be taken away, and maybe much worse will happen. We really have no choice but to obey."

Following Chief Gyasi's candid remarks, there was deep silence in the room. The only audible noise was of men breathing deeply. One man was breathing more deeply than the others were, as he was having trouble containing himself. It was Akan again. He stood up fearlessly and started waving his fist in the air as he made a traditional battle cry. He loudly swore, "I will not submit to this kind of bad governance and tyranny. I am ready to die. They can kill me and my entire family! I don't care anymore! We are better off dead than living like this with no hope for a better future."

The men sitting around Akan struggled to keep him quiet and make him sit down. It was only after much effort that they were able to calm him down and get him to take his place next to them. The other men did not like the unruly way the firebrand Akan acted, but in their heart of hearts, they understood him and deeply sympathized with his point of view. It was a matter of life and death.

The choices before them were cruel, but they would someday have to make a choice.

The chiefs looked at one another, not knowing what to say after Akan's violent outburst. Chief Yofu tried to play his role as the supreme keeper of traditions and shepherd of the villages' survival by appealing to their good sense and dedication to the welfare of their villages. In a soothing, soft-spoken tone, he said, "I know the suffering of your hearts. My heart suffers the same. But, we must do what we have to do to survive and move beyond this disheartening place on the road to our final destinies. I will ask the grandfathers for guidance. In the meantime, I ask that you do not speak of this matter. Do not forget that the president has spies everywhere. For now, stop all roadwork and dismantle the toll collection booth. I know this is hard for you, but it must be done."

That was that. The chief had spoken and it was against custom to criticize, in even the slightest manner, his decision. All knew they would have to remain silent about the content of their meeting with the chiefs. There was nothing for them to do except obey the chief without question and pray that his talk with the grandfathers would produce some promising results. They kept their mouths shut, but their depressed demeanor was more than enough to send bad vibes throughout the villages. In a flash, all the joy in the villages that had built up with all the progress they had been making dissipated. People became remorseful, hanging their heads and returning to the drudgery of absolute poverty and living hopeless lives.

From that day on, Chiefs Yofu and Gyasi camped out every night in the grandfathers' compound, sleeping on grass mats in front of the oldest grandfather's cabin door, giving many offerings to him and asking for their guidance. They poured an almost constant stream of libations on the ground in front of each grandfather's door, using the most expensive imported schnapps. They patiently waited for a sign from the grandfathers that would tell them what to do. Previously, Chief Gyasi was not a big believer in the powers of the grandfathers, but in that desperate situation he joined Chief Yofu in sincerely beseeching the grandfathers for their help.

Early one morning, they awoke to the crow of a huge red rooster standing next to them. They had never seen such a large and tall rooster before. They sat up and looked at each other, wondering if the rooster was some kind of divine sign. They turned to look at the rooster again, but it was nowhere to be seen. They found that odd, but not as odd as the next thing they would observe in front of the grandfather's door. They were looking straight at the door and placed just in front of the door was a locally made toy vehicle. That was strange indeed!

The miniature vehicle was like the ones they made from the tin peeled off sardine cans when they were children. Just as they had done many years ago, the wheels were made from discarded bottle caps. It looked like it was brand new, but it had to be old, as children no longer made such toy cars. They picked up the fragile toy to examine it closely. They agreed it had been very well made. That particular tin toy had a scoop attached in the front. At first, they did not understand that, but it finally hit them that the toy was supposed to be a bulldozer. They thought, "How ingenious!"

When their marveling over the toy diminished, it dawned on them that the toy was a sign, as it had appeared from nowhere. They looked closely into each other's eyes and exclaimed in unison, "It is a sign from the grandfathers!"

They laughed and rejoiced over the sign, but their gaiety was brought to an abrupt halt by one important question, "What does it mean?" They had no immediate answer to that key question, but they knew the village's future welfare depended on finding an answer as quickly as possible.

They excitedly entered into a very animated discussion over what the grandfathers were trying to tell them by sending a miniature toy bulldozer that was less than three inches high. They began to think about all the uses for a bulldozer. The one thing they could agree on was that bulldozers were used for roadwork. That led them to believe that somehow a bulldozer would be coming to work on their road. They knew at that moment they needed to alert the villages to prepare for the arrival of a government bulldozer. They did not understand why that was so, but they believed it was what the grandfathers were trying to tell them.

They assembled again the leaders of their two villages and related to them what the grandfathers had sent them as a sign. They backed up their words by passing the toy bulldozer around for all to see and touch. Everyone was impressed, but they were puzzled as to what they should do in terms of action. Chief Gyasi admitted, "We are as lost as you are. We are not sure what we should do about this sign. All we know is that we have to be prepared to deal with the arrival of a bulldozer."

Chief Yofu asserted, "We have given this matter much thought. We are convinced a bulldozer is coming and the grandfathers want us to do something about it. As soon as a bulldozer arrives, we must be there. I believe the grandfathers will show us what to do at that moment."

Much yammering ensued. The main upshot was that lookouts would be posted and a communications system put in place so the chiefs could be alerted to the arrival of any bulldozer. The clan heads were charged with posting a rotating series of lookouts where the road to the villages joins the main national road. If a bulldozer was arriving, the lookout would use a cow horn to alert a nearby drummer who would beat prearranged notes to be relayed by another drummer to one in the village. As soon as the first drum notes were heard in the village, the chiefs and the entire population would rush to confront the bulldozer.

One hope they had was that the bulldozer operator would be a person from their own ethnic group, as their chances of reasoning with such a person would be much better. They knew if the operator was from the president's group they would not have a chance at all. People from the president's distant ethnic group delighted in causing pain to members of the ethnic group that predominated in Ataku and Aniko. The worst thing would be the arrival of the president's uneducated soldiers who liked nothing better than to torment them and make their lives miserable.

Weeks passed, but no bulldozer appeared and people were becoming tired of all the effort the lookout system required. They were beginning to think that the grandfathers did not send the toy bulldozer and it represented a false alarm. One day when the main lookout had fallen asleep he was awakened by the loud thud of a bulldozer being unloaded from a truck in the main highway. The lookout quickly stood up and began running down the road toward the village, blowing hard on the cow horn as he dashed forward. The nearest drummer heard the bellowing horn and began madly beating his drum. The sounds of the drums traveled fast and the chiefs, with the entire population behind them, raced the five hundred yards toward the bulldozer, arriving almost before the lookout had returned to Ataku.

As soon as the chiefs saw the bulldozer, they began calling out to its driver. A small man appeared and they could see from the little scar on his cheek that he was one of their own. Happily, they greeted him and identified themselves. The man responded in the polite traditional manner, but he did not like what he saw. As far as he could see, the road was full of people. He was very troubled by that awesome sight because he had an order from the presidency to work on the road.

The chiefs explained their situation to him and begged him to leave and let them take care of their road. The man stood silently. It was very hard for him to defy traditional authority, but he replied, "I have no choice but to work on your road. It has been ordered by the president. So, please get out of the way so I can do the job the president has entrusted me."

The chiefs and all those around them did not know the bulldozer driver was not alone. Standing out of view behind the imposing bulldozer was another man from a very different part of the country. That man came out from behind the bulldozer with a menacing scowl on his face. It was obvious to the chiefs that the man was a member of the president's group, and thus, there could not be any negotiating with him. The man also wore the green khaki uniform given only to soldiers from the president's home region. The man angrily confronted the chiefs and said, "Get out of the way! This road will be worked on with you in it or off of it. Your choice."

He then turned to the driver and ordered in a threatening voice, "Get on the bulldozer, and get started with the job you have been sent here to do!"

The bulldozer driver immediately climbed up to his seat in the bulldozer and started the engine. The soldier waved at him to move forward. The driver engaged the gears and edged toward where the chiefs were standing in the middle of the road. The chiefs were gripped with fear and not sure of what they should do. Chief Yofu kept mumbling some words, asking the grandfathers for help. The bulldozer moved closer to them and the chiefs were forced to step backward. When Chief Yofu stepped back he stumbled and fell flat on the ground. Chief Gyasi saw that and thought the grandfathers had told him to lie down in front of the bulldozer, so he did the same. The chiefs' actions set off a chain reaction and in domino-fashion, all the people laid down in the road.

At that point, fear gripped the bulldozer driver. If he kept moving ahead he would crush the chiefs and many other villagers. He could not do that and gave into the strong emotions provoked by the unusual tense drama. He turned off the bulldozer and fled into the bush. The soldier also ran away, but not out of fear. He ran to get help from the nearest military station located eight miles away. Before he left, he yelled, "I will be back very soon and you will deeply regret your stupid actions!"

Lying on the ground, Chief Gyasi turned to whisper in Chief Yofu's ear. "What do we do now?"

Chief Yofu was unsure of himself but compelled by some unknown force to respond, "Everyone should stay as they are. The soldiers will be coming."

Chief Gyasi, replied, "But, that is madness. You know how cruel the soldiers are and what they will do to us."

In a very mournful voice, Chief Yofu, acknowledged, "Yes, I know we will suffer very much from beatings or worse, but we must try to hold our ground and not fight back. I feel deeply this is what we must do. Please pass the word along."

Turning to the person on his other side, Chief Gyasi said, "Pass the word that everyone must remain lying in the road until we give a sign to stand up."

One by one, the word passed to the hundreds of men, women, and children who were lying in the uncomfortable roadbed in the blazing hot sun. Except for the crying of some babies, there was only silence. Everyone was trying to build up his or her courage for the physical punishment to come from the soldiers. Many were thinking that the chief had lost his mind, but they had no choice but to obey and follow his example. There was one man, Akan, the village rebel, who was humming an old warrior's chant. He was perhaps the only one happy with what the chief was doing.

Some hours passed and they remained in the road. Many were thirsty and hungry, but they knew it was like being in war and they had to sacrifice to support their chiefs. They were perspiring heavily as the midday sun scorched them. Some fainted from dehydration. Chief Yofu sensed the suffering of his people and told Chief Gyasi to pass the word, "This is a do or die situation. We must hold our ground at any cost and be prepared to pay the ultimate price."

Those words caused even the most courageous to shed tears and shudder at the gravity of their situation. They waited for the feared enemy to arrive and bash the daylights out of them. In the distance, they could hear the muffled sound of approaching vehicles. Everyone braced themselves, as they knew it had to be the soldiers coming to do their dirty work. The soldiers arrived in two pickups. They were laughing and singing the praises of the president. They were excited by the opportunity to beat up some local villagers from a different ethnic group. They stepped out of their pickups and their sergeant ordered them to fall into formation. They marched forward as a group and halted within a few feet of the prostrate chiefs.

The scene they encountered amazed them. As far as they could see, the road was covered with bodies. It looked like a bounty of colorful rags had been deposited to cover the roadbed. They knew that in those rags were people, but they did not really care because they were not their people. They saw the people lying before them as alien forms of life that needed to be crushed. The sergeant wasted no time in giving the order for his men to fix their bayonets on their old MAS-49 French assault rifles. He hollered loudly to the chiefs lying on the ground before him, "Get up now, and have your people leave or suffer the most terrible consequences!"

The chiefs remained silent and did not flinch. The people followed the example of their chiefs. The sergeant, infuriated by that insolent behavior, ordered his men to fire shots over the people. The loud noise made by the volley of rifle fire was deafening and exceedingly frightening to all. Many babies began crying and a number of women could not help but weep openly. None of that changed anything for the heartless soldiers who were not capable of showing any pity. The sergeant gave the order to his soldiers to remove the people from the road. With their rifles in one hand and heavy knobby clubs in the other, the soldiers began to move forward to pounce on the chiefs and those around them with all their cruel might.

One very tall soldier raised his club and was about to clobber Chief Yofu when the ground under him began to shake. The earth wobbled for a moment, causing many of the soldiers to fall down. That unknown phenomenon had everyone afraid. In particular, the superstitious soldiers were overcome by fear. They interpreted the earth tremor as powerful magic for which they were no match. They began yelling at each other and demanding that their sergeant give them an order as to what to do. In their own minds, they had to escape while they could make a clean get away. The sergeant lost no time in barking loudly an order, "Depart immediately!"

The soldiers turned and ran toward their pickups. Before they could jump into their pickups, another earth tremor struck, making many of them fall down again. That would have been comical, but everyone was afraid of the strange shaking of the ground. The soldiers scrambled pell-mell into their pickups and sped off. The chiefs waited a few minutes to see if the ground had stopped

shaking before rising. They slowly stood up and dusted themselves off. The sight of the chiefs standing up provided welcome
relief to the people, who stood up and began heading silently
home. Traumatized by what had happened, the people needed
some time to recover before analyzing that day's most peculiar
events.

Chiefs Yofu and Gyasi were deeply affected and at a total loss
to explain what had happened. They knew in the days ahead
their high fetish priests would have to undertake many ceremonies in search of the answers to what had occurred that day.
They were also acutely aware that no matter what happened,
the soldiers would be back to wreak havoc on their villages. The
only thing they could do was to continue to ask the grandfathers for guidance and search for signs from the other world
as to what their next move should be. As always, they would
also ask Bobo to intervene in the other world on their behalf.
All means had to be tried to find a way out of their disastrous
predicament.

That night the people's fear and trauma increased as the
light of a brilliant full moon was made to disappear by a rare
lunar eclipse. The fact that the rare sign happened on the same
day as the earth tremor indicated to the people that powerful
forces were at work. They prayed those forces would work in
their favor. Never before had they or their grandfathers ever
seen such striking signs. They were definitely living in new and
different times.

Early the next morning a breathless messenger was pounding
on Chief Yofu's outside gate. One of his wives went to see who it
was. The man was not from their village, but spoke their dialect.
He demanded to see the chiefs immediately, saying, "I have very
important news from the capital to transmit to them."

The woman quickly responded, "Sit down on the bench next to you. I will inform the chiefs. They are sleeping near our grandfathers' houses."

The woman stepped boldly into the grandfathers' compound and spoke loudly, informing the chiefs that a man had arrived with important news from the capital. The chiefs rose and tightly wrapped around their waists their sheets of traditional cloth. They trundled off to see the man waiting for them in the adjoining compound. The man stood up when he saw the chiefs and offered his best greetings before adding, "Like many others are doing, I traveled all night on my motorbike to bring you very important news from the capital. The president is dead!"

The chiefs found it hard to believe that astounding news. They thought it probably was another one of the president's well-orchestrated ruses. Several times in the past he had faked his death in order to see what people would do. Those who were reported to him as being happy about his purported death were imprisoned and tortured. The president believed there were people permanently plotting against him, so he did his best to keep everyone off balance.

Both chiefs spoke at once the same words, "How can you be sure the president is dead?"

The man explained that a houseboy who worked in the president's palatial residence was able to escape from the palace grounds and inform the local supreme chief of what he had observed. The very nervous boy said the earthquake that had occurred upcountry caused some minor tremors in the capital. Without anyone's knowledge, the tremors had snapped the cold water pipe on the president's specially built hot water heater. The president liked taking frequent showers in super-hot water. The president also liked his booze. He was a chronic alcoholic and frequently got intoxicated on the finest whiskey money could buy. Yesterday afternoon he got into the shower when he was very inebriated and turned on the high-pressured blast of hot water he always enjoyed. While he was in the shower, the cold water pipe snapped and the president was badly scalded. He was too drunk to realize his skin was being burnt. He collapsed and the super-hot water continued to deeply scald his blubbery body.

The hot water continued to cook his body for over an hour until one of his personal bodyguards checked to see why he was taking so long in the shower. By the time the guard found him, his heart had stopped and he was very dead and terribly disfigured. The news of his macabre death was just filtering out to his inner circle and there was no doubt there would be a bitter fight over power among his cronies and sons. Rumors were spreading rapidly about his death and the people, gripped with fear, remained inside their houses, listening intently to their radios. Not a soul was seen outdoors. The capital city quickly appeared to be an empty ghost town.

The chiefs heard well what the man had told them, but they still could not bring themselves to believe the president was dead. They agreed it would be wise not to act until they were absolutely certain the president was dead. They offered the man food and drink, and a place to stay, if he needed it. But the man said. "I cannot stay. I must hurry to inform other villages."

A couple of days passed before the national radio began to broadcast martial music along with the solemn announcement that the nation's beloved President Nasungu had suddenly passed away. Nothing was said about the cause of his death and nobody knew where he had been buried. That news provided the assurance that the chiefs and all the people in the country needed to be sure the president was indeed dead. With the assurance came an explosion of joy. People celebrated massively in the streets and their homes to express their elation over the wicked president's death. Within forty-eight hours the joyous street crowds destroyed all the many photos and frescoes of the president, as well as all symbols and monuments erected for him and his hated political party. Bonfires were made to burn his many books and political treatises. The incredible size and energy of the public outburst was not lost on those vying to replace the defunct president.

In just a few days, all traces of President Nasungu's nearly forty years in power were erased by a rare and mighty explosion of spontaneous popular action. Although the people knew someone just as bad could replace him, they had seized the moment and expressed their profound hatred for the president and his party. While the internal power structure tried to sort itself out, the celebrating continued boisterously at a nonstop, around-the-clock pace for weeks. The people believed their excesses were supported by the phenomena that had occurred. They interpreted the unprecedented earthquake and the rare lunar eclipse as signs of supernatural forces at work. They believed those occult forces were on their side and supported their desperate need to be rid of such an obtuse, bloody dictator. Like in the "Wizard of Oz," a house of another kind had fallen on and killed the most-wicked one of them all.

CHAPTER THIRTEEN
MOONCHILD

Celestine's heavy pregnancy was at term. The huge bulge in her stomach had descended and her baby was overdue. She feared the consequences of having an oversized first baby. Her mother came every day to check on her and was on standby to help her deliver the baby. Celestine made various natural medicines to quicken the birth and make her strong for the rigors of childbirth. The plants and trees closely followed the progress of her pregnancy, sharing her anxiety over the big event.

As the days passed and she did not experience any labor pains, Celestine became quite concerned her baby would be too large, making it difficult to deliver naturally. She feared for her own health and the health of her baby. She would run in circles and jump up and down, hoping that would make the birthing process begin. She begged Bobo, the spirits, and the grandfathers to help her give birth, asking for her good health and that of the baby. Her situation became desperate. She was ready to do anything to provoke the birth of her child. She was in agony. She grieved and fretted about the possible consequence of a late birth. She could not wait to see her child, the son of Bobo.

Both Celestine and her mother, Evelyne, should have known that the birth of the baby had to be delayed until the next full moon, which was a very special blue moon. Upon the appearance of that brilliant full moon, it dawned on Evelyne that her grandson would be born that night. She dropped everything and discarded all her fears of the night, running to join her daughter in her forest enclave. By the time Evelyne arrived, Celestine was already in labor.

Despite her pain, Celestine warmly welcomed her mother and thanked God for her presence. They immediately agreed the baby had to be born in the light of the full moon. Evelyne cleared a spot in the middle of the compound to unroll a grass mat, which she covered with a white sheet. She fetched several buckets of water from the nearby spring and gathered some clean rags. She carefully placed on a nearby stone a small cutting knife that had been in her family for generations. That knife had been used to cut her and Celestine's umbilical cords. It was a knife blessed a hundred times over.

She instructed Celestine to lay down fully naked on her back with her legs apart to expose her entire body to the incredibly bright moon. She told her that every time the pain came she needed to push down with all her might, no matter how much it hurt. Celestine, engulfed by fear and pain, and perspiring profusely, did as her mother told her. The hours went by without much progress in giving birth to the stubborn son of Bobo. Celestine was fully dilated and the top of the baby's head could be seen, but he would not come out. Evelyne was very worried and she called to the gods for help. In particular, she called to the spirit of Bobo to intervene to save his child and the mother. Evelyne knew that it would be the death of both of them if the baby did not exit soon.

At the very moment the full moon was directly overhead, they heard a strange noise. Evelyne looked down between Celestine's legs and she was amazed to see that the baby had somehow managed to come out on his own without Celestine feeling anything. There he was! The son of Bobo was lying on the grass mat with his eyes wide open, smiling at the full moon and making muffled cooing sounds of happiness. He had not cried, but seemed just fine. Evelyne shouted praises and exclaimed, "Daughter, behold, your son is born. He is so beautiful!"

Upon hearing those words, tears flooded Celestine's eyes. Evelyne very carefully picked up the big and well-formed white baby, laying him on Celestine's stomach. Celestine was overcome by joy when she saw her baby for the first time. Evelyne handed the cutting knife to Celestine and pulled up the section of the umbilical cord that had to be cut. It was the traditional duty of every mother to cut the umbilical cords of their babies. Celestine swiftly cut the cord and her mother placed the remaining cord between Celestine's legs and waited for the afterbirth to come out. She handed Celestine a damp cloth so she could begin cleaning her baby. She also gave Celestine some herbal medicine that she had previously prepared to rub on her vagina to reduce the pain and any chance of infection.

Evelyne collected the afterbirth and buried it in a hole on the compound that she had dug days ago. That hole would be clearly marked with a large stone. The afterbirth was considered part of a person, and thus, deserving respect and a proper burial. Evelyne returned to her daughter and found her sitting up, already breastfeeding her hungry infant. It was something of a miracle that Celestine's overinflated breasts were already able to produce the milk and the rich colostrum her baby needed to get a healthy start in life. Celestine startled her mother with a painful yelp, saying,

"How can my baby already have teeth? When he bites my nipples it really hurts."

Evelyne spoke softly, her heart bursting with love for her daughter. "Let me hold the baby while you clean yourself. I need to show fully your child to the moon." She gently lifted the baby into the air and held it high above her head in the direction of the full moon. She slowly turned around so every side of the baby would be seen by the moon and penetrated by its light. She knew that a "moonchild" needed to be shown to the full moon for its appreciation and to establish a bond between the child and the moon that would last for all time.

Celestine watched what her mother was doing with her baby and understood she had given birth to a moonchild, and that his name would therefore be "Letivi," meaning beloved offspring of the moon. As he was also born in the first minutes of a Tuesday, just like his father Bobo, he would also have the name of Bokuma, meaning roughly, "the Tuesday son of a Tuesday man." Celestine would also give him the Christian name, David. Celestine was perhaps the only person in the country who knew that David was the real name of Bobo.

Evelyne said a few words. "I will stay with you, my darling daughter, until the first rays of the sun, and then I must rush home to tell your father the good news. I will be coming every day to check on you and to see if you need anything. I will tell your helper, Leon, to not disturb you until you send word for him to come." They passed the night quietly except for the sweet cooing of Letivi. At first light, Evelyne left mother and child sleeping and returned to her home in Aniko.

She arrived breathless and exhausted at her home, but she could not lose any time in informing her husband, Chief Gyasi, of the birth of his grandson. She found her husband at that early hour already in his modest office sitting at his desk. She could not contain her joy, "Gyasi, my husband, you have a healthy grandson named Letivi. Your daughter gave birth to a moonchild in the middle of the night. He is the son of Bobo. Both baby and mother are doing fine."

Chief Gyasi knew his daughter was pregnant and due to give birth, but he had only reluctantly accepted that her baby was Bobo's son. But, when confronted with the birth of his grandson, he could only respond, "My dear wife, this great news makes me very happy. I accept the birth of Bobo's son as a great blessing. It is very important and precious having Bobo's offspring among us. This is such exciting news. I must share it first with my brother, Chief Yofu, before anyone else learns of Bobo's child. I will go immediately to tell Yofu. In the meantime, remain quiet on this subject."

Gyasi strode quickly the five hundred yards separating his village from Ataku and climbed briskly the additional hundred yards up the lower western slope of Mount Ataku to Yofu's compound. While he was very happy for the birth of his new grandson, he knew the fact that he was Bobo's son would be something to handle with the greatest of care. Having Bobo's son among them was a big deal, with ramifications in the earthly world and the spirit world.

Yofu's door was always open for Gyasi. Nonetheless, Gyasi clapped twice and identified himself. Yofu immediately responded, "Please enter." At the same time, he asked the others who were with him to leave the room. Yofu was always happy to see Gyasi. Smiling he said, "Welcome my brother. What news do you bring?"

Gyasi lost no time, "My dear older brother, I just received the good news that my daughter Celestine gave birth to a healthy son last night under the light of the full moon. I must tell you that without a doubt we know it is Bobo who fathered this child."

Yofu trusted Gyasi 100 percent, but the magnitude of that earth-shaking news prompted him to blurt out, "Are you sure this is the son of Bobo? If so, this has many troubling aspects."

Gyasi confirmed, "Yes, it is the half-caste child of Bobo." He went on to explain how his daughter had been chosen to replace Mama Atiwono and learned tree language that permitted her to communicate with the old baobab, which made the spirit of Bobo appear before his wife and daughter. Bobo's spirit confirmed he was indeed the father. He also reminded the chief of the rare rainy day during the last dry season and told him that was when the child was conceived.

Chief Yofu was having a hard time digesting the momentous news. He did not know how to respond, but he did know the news about the birth of Bobo's son had to be kept secret in order to preserve tranquility in the villages. After a few minutes of agonized pondering, Yofu conveyed his initial thinking, "Brother Gyasi, this is an event of huge proportions and many complications that we must analyze carefully before saying anything to anyone. Let us keep this a secret until we have had the opportunity to determine the best course we should follow in the aftermath of this unprecedented historical event. This could be a real turning point for our villages."

Chief Gyasi nodded and grunted his strong agreement with Yofu's interim conclusion and said, "I will instruct my wife to not mention this birth to anyone. I will tell her to tell my daughter that we are keeping this a secret for now. There is the problem of my daughter's helper, Leon."

Chief Yofu jumped in and said, "Let us summon Leon and give him instructions to keep secret the birth of this child. We will threaten him with the worst kinds of punishment if he does not do as he is told. Now, let us begin examining closely the impact on our communities if it is known that Bobo's son is among us."

It became apparent to both of them that if people knew Bobo's son was among them he would be thronged by well-wishers from the entire district. That would not be good for Celestine and her work, or for the raising of the child. Knowing a son of a spirit lived among them would be very disruptive and divert people's focus away from the kind of progress they were trying to achieve in their two villages. The son of Bobo would be treated like a demigod, and thus, he would not be able to assume any useful leadership role.

It would be much preferred, and in the best interest of their villages, if Letivi was raised in a way that prepared him for future leadership roles. They knew achieving the progress needed to lift their people out of poverty required competent and honest leaders to inspire their people on to greater things. If prepared in the right way, Bobo would be a great leader for the next generation.

The two chiefs agreed to sleep overnight on the weighty subject and resume their discussion the next morning. In the meantime, Chief Yofu would consult the grandfathers and send his guards to fetch Leon. Gyasi reconfirmed he would make sure his wife and daughter did not mention the birth of the child to anyone. As they separated, both were seeing for the first time that it was a much bigger subject than they had anticipated. It was much clearer that it was a matter with the potential to make or break the future of their two villages.

Both chiefs slept little that night as they pondered all the options related to the birth of Bobo's son. Chief Yofu slept in front of the oldest grandfather's cabin, asking for guidance on what should be done about Bobo's son. They also called upon the spirit of Bobo for his advice. By the time they met again the following morning, they were exhausted and their heads were suffering from an overload of thoughts on the critical subject.

They sat together for almost an hour in Chief Yofu's private meetinghouse without either one saying a word. Yofu broke the silence with a striking statement. "I am getting old and I have nobody to replace me. Ever since our encounter with the government's bulldozer, my heart has not functioned well. I fear that my days are numbered." He did not admit that all of that had come to him in a short, but vivid dream where he could hear the grandfathers talking in their ancient dialect.

Chief Gyasi was shocked and deeply moved by those words and retorted, "My dear older brother, please do not talk like that. You are needed on this Earth for many years to come. Your work here is not yet done."

"I wish it were otherwise, but I have now been chief for nearly forty years and it is time to pass this responsibility on to a selected replacement. We must ensure a good future for our villages by preparing a smooth transition of power and responsibility to a new generation of leaders." Upon saying those words, Chief Yofu hung his head and made a sound that conveyed to Gyasi that he was speaking truths that had to be accepted.

A profoundly troubled Gyasi reluctantly accepted Yofu's words and wondered aloud, "Your sad words pain me, but I must ask how this relates to the son of Bobo and the purpose of our discussion today."

Yofu lifted his head and stared straight into Gyasi's eyes and firmly asserted, "The son of Bobo will be our chief one day. This has been communicated to me by the grandfathers. I see it as a fact that we must accept and for which we must prepare. We must trust and obey this instruction from the grandfathers."

Gyasi was speechless. He had not expected that alternative. After some deep reflection, the only words Gyasi could muster were, "So be it!" He saw no sense in arguing the point. The only thing left was for Gyasi and Yofu to map out how the succession would take place.

Yofu started by saying, "My replacement must be of royal clan blood, so I will claim your grandson as my own son. You must convince your wife and daughter of the wisdom of this decision and the absolute need to keep this secret with them forever. They should easily see that this decision is in the best interests of all concerned."

Gyasi could do nothing but listen to Yofu communicate the outlines of his plan. Yofu continued, "I will concoct a story that the light-skinned Letivi is the product of the liaison I had with a daughter of a half-caste woman and a Whiteman who lived in the capital city. I will say that I saw this woman every time I traveled to Melomti."

Yofu continued to rollout key elements of his big plan, "As soon as Letivi is old enough, he must be sent to the capital city and begin attending the best schools, starting with kindergarten. Your daughter must accept this arrangement. She will always be the only real mother who Letivi recognizes and loves, but Letivi is for all of us."

Gyasi was struggling to digest the broad scope of Yofu's master plan. It was good that Yofu took long pauses between presenting each main element of his plan, as that gave Gyasi time to reflect on each part. Yofu was not finished. "When I die, you will serve as regent until Letivi can take on the role as residing chief of our two villages. Yes, my dear younger cousin, I said our two villages. We must begin now, working to join our villages into the one village they should have always been."

Words were slow to come out of Gyasi's mouth. He had been swept away by the depth and breadth of Yofu's plan. After a long pause and much thought, Gyasi could only say, "It is taking me some time to consider and adjust to all that you have said. I am seeing the wisdom of all you have put forth, and nothing incites objection on my part. I can see that it will be a challenge to put your plan into action, but I also see it is a challenge we must meet if we are going to build a better future for our people."

Both men stood, shook hands, and embraced each other. They understood in the depths of their beings that from that day on they would be leading their people to a new and better future. They were convinced their vision of the future was the right one, and henceforth, they would work so that all the villagers would share their vision. With a clear vision and well-defined milestones for progressing from where they were at the time to where they wanted to be in the distant future, they believed success could be achieved. They were thankful for the birth of the son of Bobo. They were thankful that the moonchild had already shown them a better way forward.

CHAPTER FOURTEEN
POWER STRUGGLE

High tension gripped the country. The people were exceedingly happy over the death of their hated dictator, but extremely uneasy about who would replace him. The country had come to a standstill as people waited to learn who would be their next president. There was not any clear succession plan. Each of the dozen men who had been close to the dead president believed he should replace him. Those corrupt cronies of the defunct President Nasungu met secretly in the dining room of the mansion the former president kept within the military barracks in Melomti. Each one of those egotistical men believed the meeting would result in his selection as the country's new president.

Hamma believed he was the one most favored because he was the closest to the former president. He also had the most power and wealth. When the meeting started, Hamma ordered everyone to be quiet and announced with much confidence in his voice, "I believe it is obvious to all of you that I am the one to be your new president."

After that unanticipated announcement, the room became very quiet. All eyes stared incredulously at Hamma who was waiting to hear a unanimous acclamation of his self-nomination. Sitting opposite the table from Hamma was the dead president's most educated son, Elias, who had come home from his studies in Europe. The urbane man got up from his chair, walked around the table to where Hamma was standing, looked him in the eye and violently slapped him in the face and yelled, "You bastard fool, sit down and remain quiet. You have no business speaking here. This is a family matter."

Hamma immediately fell into his chair and hung his head like a beaten dog. Elias remained on his feet, and then turned to the group and said, "Let's get serious here. I am the best qualified to replace my father. Now, we should easily be able to agree quickly and announce my nomination to the public."

Some people in the room were ready to side with Elias. But others were reluctant to join him, as they did not know him. Elias had spent most of his life abroad going to expensive boarding schools. In fact, that was the first time most of those in the room had ever seen him. One of those who sided with Elias spoke in favor of his nomination. Others were trying to see which way the wind was blowing before deciding whether they should tie their future fortunes to Elias' bandwagon. All wanted to get the matter over with as quickly as possible, but they also wanted to make sure they were making the right decision. They knew very well that their future fortunes and lives depended on the outcome of the meeting.

Elias' younger brother, Rafael, was in a nervous state. He was very uncomfortable, as he was unaccustomed to being in the capital and participating in such meetings as that one. The former president had kept Rafael in his home village upcountry because he wanted one of his children instructed in the old, traditional ways. He also needed someone he could trust in his home area to keep him informed of events there. Rafael had only a primary school education, but he was not dumb. He knew well the ways of his ethnic group and how his father's roots in that group had helped him stay in power for decades. Rafael was no less corrupt than the others were, but he was more clever and willing to compromise with the times. The usually very quiet Rafael loudly cleared his voice and said, "I think we should have a brief break of less than an hour so everyone can think about this important subject. We can come back after a break and make our decision." Those assembled breathed a collective sigh of relief and loudly agreed with Rafael.

The group returned to the meeting room at the appointed hour following a cordial coffee break. They took their places around the table while Elias remained standing. Everyone, except Elias' brother, Rafael, who had excused himself to go to the toilet, was in place. Once all were comfortably seated and Elias had their attention, he stated, "I see my brother is not here, but that is not important. I assume that all of you are in agreement with naming me our country's new president. If anyone objects, they can say so now."

Just when Elias was ready to acclaim himself as president, the double doors to the meeting room were forcefully thrown open with a loud clack and a dozen well-armed soldiers came bursting into the room at a brisk trot. The group was in shock. Before any of them could utter a word, they were roughly assembled and herded out the door. Members of the group demanded to know why they were being treated in such a brutal fashion. The soldiers did not say a word and roughly tossed their captives into a waiting military truck, which quickly sped off. The truck drove all day and night to a prison camp located in the most remote part of the country. Except for their close family members, they would not be missed and nobody would care what happened to them. For sure, their careers were over, if not their lives too.

That evening Rafael appeared on national TV and radio to announce to the public that he had been named the interim president. He explained, "I know all of you are weary of my father's long reign and the excesses of his regime. It is therefore my intention to remain president only as long as it takes to organize democratic elections. I believe the people should be free to elect a president of their choosing. It is now acceptable for political parties to form and put forth their candidates."

The people could not believe what they were hearing from the young man. What he was saying was much better than anything they could have imagined. After all those years, they were finally getting what they had dreamed of having: democracy. Those with a political bent began immediately setting up a party. They brought together those they could trust to be part of their party's governing board. No matter that all those people came from their home area and the same ethnic group. Dozens of aspiring political leaders formed their parties overnight. Within two weeks, over one hundred political parties had been declared.

For President Rafael, the chaotic formation of a huge number of political parties was just what he expected. Deep down, Rafael was a very astute and keen observer of the people in his country. He wanted the same thing as his father: absolute power for as many years as possible. His approach was to give the people what they asked for. He knew in advance that the people were not capable of developing a majority consensus about anything. The leaders of the people were also easily manipulated by bribes and it was easy to play one against another. He was counting on the people's inability to get their act together. He was intent on showing a nice external face, but his real objective was to enjoy the same impunity and longevity that his father had while enriching himself.

Rafael's appearance helped him deceive the people. Although he was hard as steel inside, he looked like an innocent young man who was sincerely unhappy with the way his father had ruled. He gathered around him a group of advisors representing every area of the country. He gave them lucrative positions and paid them exorbitant salaries. He knew if he could corrupt them and keep them happy, it would be in their vested interests to keep him in power. In that way, Rafael garnered the support of all the political and traditional elites in the country. They all worked together to make more money for themselves and their families. Making money was their religion and the almighty "dollar" always trumped doing what was right. He also knew that he could always keep the people sufficiently content if he kept food prices low, particularly the price of corn meal, the major food staple.

The concept of nation building was an alien one. Taking care of your family and ensuring their good future was everything. It was always family before country, which was nothing more than an artificial creation of the colonial powers. National boundaries cut through villages and ethnic groups in a random manner. It was as if the colonial powers had been blindfolded when they divided Africa into countries. A favorite comment of the people on that old subject was, "You cannot divide people like you are cutting a loaf of bread."

Perhaps even more important to maintaining Rafael in power was that he had the support of the military leaders. All the key leaders of the military were of his ethnic group and hailed from his home area. While growing up in his native village, Rafael developed close relationships with those military leaders and their families. The day after his succession to power, Rafael doubled the salaries of all military officers. That was all very important to his strategy of staying in power; but even more important was his holding of the keys to the main national army munitions storage dump located just outside his northern village.

His father could not trust anyone, so he had secretly entrusted Rafael with the keys to that strategic and well-guarded building. His father knew very well that soldiers would have a hard time overthrowing him by force if they did not have the keys to the remote dump. Many soldiers did not have any bullets for their guns and those who did had very few. Rafael was intent on controlling the ballots and the bullets. In reality, the munitions dump held the future of the country, and in many ways the country was hostage to the military.

Rafael skillfully co-opted all the main political and military leaders across the country. He made them happy and they could not help but sing Rafael's praises. He managed to pull the wool over everyone's eyes. Happiness spread across the country. It was hard to argue with more money in your pocket. Rafael had his chief governance advisors devise a decentralization project that received the backing of major foreign donors, thus elevating his status with them. That project would create independent elected bodies at the district and community levels and involve traditional chiefs with government decision-making that concerned their villages. Each elected representative and chief would receive a government stipend. Rafael's hidden agenda was to extend corruption down to the grass roots level and make people dependent on his vision and largesse. A little money could go a long way among such desperately poor people.

While Chiefs Yofu and Gyasi were happy with President Rafael and his many initiatives, they remained leery of anything coming from the central government. They gave Rafael high marks because people like Hamma were no longer around to threaten them. They had qualms about receiving government stipends, but it would not be good to refuse free money. They decided that their stipends would be donated in a very above board and transparent manner to their community development fund. That would help raise the money they needed to achieve many projects they envisioned for their villages. Mostly, the chiefs wanted to be left alone by the central government and to be allowed to pursue as they pleased their own development activities.

One project they were keen to start as soon as possible was a scholarship fund for the brightest students graduating from local primary schools. They had noted over the years that it was not the quality of the building that produced good students but the quality of the teaching. Very committed teachers taught some of the best students under big shade trees. They were increasingly insisting on good teachers and getting rid of those teachers who did not perform well. They also set up a parent-teacher association to oversee the management of the schools.

They were particularly concerned that promising graduates from their primary schools stayed in the villages, as they did not have the means to go to a town that had a secondary school. The purpose of the scholarship fund was to support those students so they could finish secondary school and maybe go on to gain university degrees. Everyone knew that to land a good job you needed higher education. Having more of their children educated at a higher level was perceived as a good investment, as having a paid job meant more money for the villages. All the people from the villages who had jobs in other places sent remittances back to their families in the villages. Those remittances were often an important percentage of a household's disposal income.

If more youths got jobs, the better it was for the villages. The departure of youths from the villages also reduced the number of mouths to feed and pressure on available farmland. Some villagers believed they should pool all their resources in the scholarship fund so that top students could be sent to Europe or America for university training. Maybe the best development strategy for the villages was to train their youths for well-paying jobs in other countries. When many youths were gainfully employed they could also contribute to the scholarship fund. Another benefit of such a scheme was when the youths would visit and share what they learned with the entire village. Some of the more successful youths made enough money to build their retirement homes in the villages and invest in village improvement activities.

The scholarship fund also encouraged students to study more diligently in hopes that they could win a scholarship. Some students said they could do better if they had more time to study. In particular, they had trouble studying at night by candlelight. They wished electrical lights could be installed so they could study more easily at night. When the chiefs became aware of the expressed need for electrical lights, they recalled the project Bobo had proposed to them to provide water and some electricity. They had turned down that project because they could not collaborate at the time, and they did not want to disturb the night with electrical lights. The interest expressed by the students in having electrical light to study at night forced them to revisit Bobo's ingenious project.

They had always thought that rebuilding the school Bobo had built, but that had been destroyed by Aniko's jealousy, was the top priority. But then, they were thinking that the water and electricity generation project was a higher priority. The students needed light more than they needed bricks and mortar. They designated a group of people to serve on a committee to resurrect Bobo's ideas and lay out useable plans for implementing the promising project. The committee was asked to report back to the chiefs within two months.

With their almost daily discussions about what their villages needed the most, the views of the chiefs began to change and they began to see the priority needs of their villages in a different light. They could see that, if their people were not healthy and well nourished, they could not be productive and fulfill their full potential. Clean water and good sanitation were, therefore, essential basics. But, none of that would be any good if one did not get a good start in life. That meant mothers and their babies had to have good care and be well fed.

Slowly, they started piecing together a development strategy for their villages that gave priority to focusing on satisfying basic human needs. They gave top priority to Bobo's water project, which would pipe clean water down the mountain slope to the villages. That project would not only reduce waterborne diseases, but it would relieve women of the heavy and time-consuming burden of hauling water. The chiefs believed women could use the time saved to take better care of their children and grow more nutritious vegetables in their compound gardens. They could see the key to better nutrition was to increase the quantity and variety of vegetables cultivated by women. They believed the compound garden was a big part of the answer to their development woes.

The chiefs continued to insist they could not achieve higher health standards as long as people continued to defecate in the bush. A central theme of the chief's development plan was the construction of a latrine for each family and larger community latrines in each neighborhood. They also saw that each school needed a latrine. In every instance, they saw building separate latrines for men and women as necessary. And, with each latrine, there needed to be a hand washing station. They were convinced that regular hand washing with soap was essential to avoid infections and to reduce the transmission of diseases.

The chiefs summoned their people to present to them their basic development strategy and rationale for the villages. Chief Yofu summed up their development program with the following words, "Water, latrines, vegetables, and hand washing. And, with the water there will be the light the students need to work on their studies at night."

Chief Gyasi had prepared some remarks. "We must first focus on a handful of priorities and achieve success with a few key objectives before moving on to other development activities. Development is a process that starts with small steps and then leads to more complicated phases once the capacity and resources are available to tackle more. We cannot rush the process. A solid foundation must be built and we need to move from one success to another. Our success will depend on all of us working together harmoniously and committing ourselves strongly to the objectives we set for ourselves. There can be no turning back. With each passing day, we must always move a step closer to a better life for each of us, our children, and future generations. There is no room for laziness!"

Chief Yofu had more to say, "I would like to add to my brother's good words. We all know that life is much more expensive now and we have become too many. We must start thinking "quality" and not "quantity." We need to manage, in a much better way, the scarce resources we have. We are living in times that require we stop all bad habits and negative traditions that impede our progress. We spend too much money on nonproductive things. We have to be more careful about how we invest our money. For example, we spend too much for funerals, marriages, and visits to healers and fetish priests. That is money we should invest in our children and other things that improve our lives. Most of all, we must rid ourselves of superstitions that hold us back. It is well that we worship the grandfathers, spirits, and all our traditional gods, but this should not cause us to sacrifice our progress in these new times. We need to harness our beliefs and direct ourselves toward activities that help us create a more resilient and better place to live. We must open our minds and change our attitudes. Our biggest enemy is our own ignorance."

Those were powerful new words that the people were not accustomed to hearing from their leaders. Many people were overwhelmed to hear their chiefs talk like that. The people did not understand what the chiefs were trying to say. A long discussion ensued among the people and many questions were raised and answered by the chiefs. The chiefs observed that much awareness-raising was needed to enable the villagers to buy into their project ideas. It was clear to them that there was a need for capacity building and that a learning process had to accompany the development process. People needed to become thoroughly versed in the projects so they could consider them as their own projects. All the people needed to buy into the process and take ownership of the process, and feel deeply that they were in control and responsible for its success or failure. The people did not know it, but they were truly on their way to becoming the masters of their own destinies. There was a long road ahead, but a new day was dawning.

CHAPTER FIFTEEN
UNIFICATION

Chief Yofu surprised himself by living longer than he expected. He was happy that he had been able to live for a few more years and help oversee all the good progress being made by the villages. It was an exciting and gratifying time to be living in the villages. New cacao plants were being regularly distributed and planted. New hygiene and sanitation practices had made the villages the cleanest in the country. Very soon the water and light project would be finished. Primary school graduates were garnering the top national test scores in the country. Many benefited from scholarships and found good jobs that permitted them to send money home. The levels of happiness and hope for a better future had never been higher.

The central government was no longer a burden. People did not really like the new president, Rafael, but he was such an improvement over his father that complaints were few. The main thing was the central government left the villages alone so they could pursue their own homemade development schemes. That was really all the people wanted. The people were pleased that

President Rafael's half-baked decentralization schemes were easily manageable and they had the flexibility to use the funds provided to their elected local leaders as they pleased. The central government readily observed that the best help they could provide was to stay out of the way and not give any help unless requested to do so.

President Rafael could see that sometimes the best aid of all was no aid. The experience demonstrated by Ataku and Aniko led President Rafael to develop a new policy that was centered on a philosophy of self-reliance and solidarity. He gave speeches throughout the country encouraging villages to achieve as much progress as they could on their own without any dependence on external aid. In his speeches, he would often cite what had happened in Ataku and Aniko as good examples to follow. His speeches caused many people to travel to Ataku and Aniko to see for themselves what was going on in the two villages. Many went back to their own villages to replicate what they saw in Ataku and Aniko. Progressively, the spin-off effect from the achievements of Ataku and Aniko were positively impacting the entire country. Both Chiefs Yofu and Gyasi became famous throughout the country and President Rafael bestowed upon them the highest honor of the country: the National Knighthood Medal for outstanding public service. They were indeed the genuine heroes of their times.

Of course, President Rafael really did not believe in what he said, but he liked the policy and convincing rationale of self-reliance because that meant he could keep more government funds for himself. The chiefs and almost everybody in the country knew that President Rafael was not sincere, but that was okay with them as long as he did not bring any harm or interference their way. They were willing to live and cooperate with the veneer of democracy with which the president was trying to paint the country, as long as they were allowed to pursue greater economic prosperity and happiness in their own way. In other words, they were agreeable to pretending they had democracy if that made the president happy and allowed them to do as they pleased. For the people, the ability to pursue, unhindered, higher prosperity trumped all other concerns.

Chief Yofu felt he had been living on borrowed time and that made him want to move as quickly as possible on to the final phase of his succession plan. The first step in that plan was to gain a consensus of the unification of the two villages into one village under a single chief. The next step would be to reach an agreement with Chief Gyasi on serving as cochiefs until the death of one of them. Then the remaining chief would serve as a regent until a new chief could be identified and placed on the throne. The chiefs had discussed all of those matters many times, and they were in complete agreement on every point. They had to gain a consensus among senior elders and clan heads in both villages. The only thing remaining to do after that would be to ask for the blessing of the grandfathers.

The criers went out to every point in the villages and clanged loudly their iron gong-gongs, announcing to the people that all elders and clan heads were summoned to an important meeting the next day one hour after first light in Chief Yofu's large courtyard within his compound. Those men rose before daylight and prepared themselves to be at Chief Yofu's compound at the appointed hour. They silently walked along the villages' dirt paths as the early morning sun cast long shadows to the west. At every juncture, groups would form and continue walking deliberately in a single file toward the chief's house. They gathered in front of the chief's compound and waited to be told to enter. It was an odd sight to see fifty or so men, dressed in their best traditional clothes, remain silent while huddled closely together in the cramped space allowed by the narrow passageway.

One of the chief's guards appeared and barked out an instruction to enter. The oldest entered first, followed by the chiefs of the oldest clans. The last to enter was the chief of a clan that was the last to be established many years ago. There were grass mats spread on the ground under the chief's big straw-covered circular hangar. As there were not enough benches for such a large group, all would be sitting on the grass mats. They removed their shoes and sandals and left them at the entrance before taking a place on the grass mats. In the front would be the senior elders followed by clan chiefs, beginning with the oldest clan and ending in the back row with the youngest clan. Two chief chairs were placed in front for Yofu and Gyasi. They would, of course, face that group of the most important men in their villages.

All the men remained silent while they found their places on the mats and sat down on the ground. When the chiefs were told that all men were present, they made their entrance. Upon their arrival, all men stood to show respect for their chiefs. The chiefs took their seats and the men sat down as before. Both chiefs were dressed in their finest traditional clothes and carried with them their ornamental chief canes. Chief Yofu opened the meeting by tapping his cane five times on the hard ground.

Following that traditional tapping of the royal cane, Chief Gyasi announced in a loud voice so all could easily hear him, "My older brother, Chief Yofu, will speak first. I ask all of you to listen attentively without interruption to the very important words he has for you."

Chief Yofu took several minutes before speaking. He looked around the meeting place and tried to make solid eye contact with each man who was present. Each man could see that Chief Yofu had become old and weary. Most notable was the sadness in his face. Chief Yofu's demeanor made it very clear to each man that the words he would pronounce were weighing very heavily upon him. The level of seriousness and sadness communicated by Chief Yofu's sorrowful countenance was contagious, making the mood of all present deeply somber.

"My time is nearing its end," Chief Yofu said in a soft, throaty, but clearly audible voice.

"I must now convey to you my desires for my succession. I have been your chief for forty years and in these days and times we must still follow our traditions and wait for my death before worrying about replacing me. I ask for your deepest empathy with what I have to tell you."

Chief Yofu paused before continuing. He raised his voice an octave and said unequivocally, "We can no longer be two villages. We have been working together for several years as one village and we must become forever one village. Thanks to Bobo's miraculous transformation, we have put behind us the nonsense of our ancient feud that held us back for nearly three generations. We cannot afford to lose any more time. We must be one village under one chief."

All the men followed closely his every word, nodding their agreement until his last sentence, which caused a halt in their thinking and a collective look of bewilderment. They were also asking themselves, "How could there be one chief when there are two sitting before us?"

At that point, Chief Gyasi, intervened, "Yes, one chief and that chief is the most senior chief sitting before you. Chief Yofu has been a chief for forty years. His father had been chief for forty years before him. His grandfather was a chief while we were all in one village on top of the mountain. We must be one village again under one chief. Why not? We are all descendants of the same grandfathers and related by blood. We are all Atakuans, people of the mountain."

The profound nature of what they were hearing had all the men looking at each other with inquiring faces to see if anyone would speak up. They felt like they should say something, but the logic of what the chiefs were saying was so undeniable they were lost for words.

Chief Yofu picked up where Gyasi had left off. "I propose that from this day forth we are all Atakuans and Aniko will become one important part of Ataku. My brother, Chief Gyasi, will be a cochief with me until my death, and then he will serve as a regent until one of my children becomes old and prepared enough to sit on the royal stool."

The men assembled were struggling to digest and appreciate the weighty information. They were hoping the chiefs would call a brief recess so they could confer with one another, but Chief Yofu indicated he had more to say.

"My fellow Atakuans, I have some important things to add. I already know who I want to replace me. I have a young son you do not know. You know the children I have in the village, but you do not know those who live outside the village. I have one son who is very gifted, and I see him as the best one to replace me when he becomes of age. I believe strongly that he has all the natural leadership abilities needed to lead our village to bigger and better things. His name is Letivi and I had him with a light-skinned woman who lives in the capital. I intend to introduce him to you soon."

Chief Yofu's admittance that he had a son with a woman in the capital was easily accepted by all, as it was quite common for men to have children with women they met when they traveled. Many men at the meeting had children living elsewhere. Usually children would live with their mothers until the age of reason, which was generally about seven years of age. At that age they would go and live with their fathers.

"I have one other important point to add," interjected Chief Yofu. "I leave this instruction for you to adhere to when I die. I command you not to do the usual very lavish and expensive chief's funeral for me. For me, that is a waste of money that could be used for more productive purposes. Too much money is spent in the village for baptisms, marriages, and funerals. It is better to use this money for our children's education. I hope my example will lead all of you to do the same."

The order by the chief not to organize a big funeral for him was shocking. It caused much murmuring to ensue. They could not argue with his logic, but what he asked was such a profound change in their traditional custom that it would be very hard to practice. They could not imagine not having a traditional funeral for him as all chiefs had previously been afforded.

The most senior clan head felt compelled to say something and asked to be recognized. He said mostly the obvious, "I, for one, applaud all that you propose. I only wish to remind you that for any of this to happen you need the support of the majority of us. I also note for all present that the naming of a chief is a matter for the senior elders of the royal family and the selection of a new chief must meet the approval of a majority of clan heads. I see it as your choice to have a funeral or not. We have noted that you have opted for a simple funeral. Thank you for giving me the opportunity to speak."

Chief Gyasi jumped back into the discussion by saying, "Let's not waste time. All those in favor with what we are proposing raise your right hand."

The men were not accustomed to taking important action so quickly, but it was hard for them not to do as their chiefs asked. Slowly, and with a bit of hesitation, the men began lifting their right hands until all hands were raised.

Chief Gyasi spoke again, "We thank each and every one of you for listening well to what we had to say and for agreeing with us. Please report to your families what has been decided here this morning. We are convinced that these decisions are necessary if we are to maintain and accelerate progress in our village. Long live Atakuans!"

The chiefs rose and exited the meeting space. As they left the group, the men applauded loudly. It was an exciting moment and all were very happy about being unified as one village. With the divisions that once separated them obliterated, they were fully united and ready to achieve great things together. They left the room chanting loudly, "One village, one chief!" They kept chanting as a group and individually until they returned to their respective home compounds. By the time the chanting ceased, everyone in the village knew about unification.

CHAPTER SIXTEEN
WHITE CHIEF

Chief Gyasi had his work cut out for him. He had to explain to his wife, Evelyne, and his daughter Celestine, the necessity of arranging things so Letivi would replace Chief Yofu as supreme chief. It was not easy to create and perpetuate a lie of such huge proportions, but doing so was in the best interest of the community and the welfare of future generations. They had to work together without misstep to falsify history so their people could enjoy a better future. The truth was of little importance compared to the survival and well-being of a people.

Evelyne readily understood. She was very pleased that her grandson was destined to become the chief of Ataku. The job of convincing Celestine of the wisdom of making her son supreme chief was given to Evelyne. She had the habit of visiting her daughter, Celestine, almost every other day. Early one morning she arrived in Celestine's secluded forest enclave and called her name. She first said, "Celestine, my daughter, I am here." Then she said in a more formal tone, "Mama Atibona, your mother has arrived."

Celestine would usually reply, "I am here with my plants. I'm coming."

As soon as Letivi would hear his grandmother's voice, he would run to her and hug her tightly. Letivi was five-years-old and had already shown signs of being very intelligent and wise beyond his years. He was a natural tree talker and learned well under his mother's tutelage about the purpose of every plant. He was a beautiful, well-built boy, physically big for his age. He had rusty brown hair that fell around his head in large curls. His greenish-colored eyes had a magnetic effect on all those who looked into them. His golden brown complexion made him appear as someone from another place. To the local population he would be perceived as white.

After greeting his grandmother, he would ask her if she had any news of his father, Bobo. Letivi knew that his father was a Whiteman who was swallowed by the ancient baobab and transformed into a spirit who remained among them in the other world. He also knew that his grandmother frequently took offerings to the old baobab and said prayers, asking for information related to Bobo and giving news about Bobo's son, Letivi. Evelyn tried to visit the old baobab every full moon, as she knew that was the time she was most likely to receive news about Bobo.

Evelyne gave Letivi her usual response, "My darling child, I go all the time to the old baobab, but it has not yet revealed to me its secrets about your father. My dear moonchild, please keep the faith. Some day we will know all we need to know. The main thing now is to keep yourself healthy and strong, as you have a great destiny ahead of you."

Celestine arrived and sat next to her mother in their usual places on an old mahogany log. Evelyne indicated she had something important to say and it was best that Letivi leave them alone for a short while. "Letivi, please go ask those new plants I was working with if they need more water and make sure all the plants have all they need."

Upon hearing his mother's words, Letivi dutifully sped off to do as he was instructed. The plants and trees loved Letivi and enjoyed talking to him. He made them laugh and they often teased him and pulled jokes on him. Letivi considered it quite natural to converse with all living things. He was not aware that in the outside world that was not the case. He had never gone far from his mother's camp, and his mother constantly told him that he must stay near her.

Evelyne began softly by saying, "My dear daughter, your child grows much with each passing day. Soon he must go to school. Your father and Chief Yofu have decided the important status of your child requires that he go to the best schools in the capital."

"Mother, I know my son is very intelligent and he should benefit from the best schooling. It will be hard for me to live without him, but it is best for him to go away to school. I hope he can spend all his holidays with me. The plants and trees are really attached to him."

Evelyne breathed a slight sigh of relief to hear her daughter accept without argument her son going away to school. Her daughter's agreeable response encouraged her to continue. "Daughter, there is more I must tell you. The chiefs see your son as the one who will replace Chief Yofu and serve as the supreme leader of all chiefs in the district."

Celestine gasped when she heard that and quickly interjected, "How can my son replace Chief Yofu? He is not a blood descendant of the royal family. This is not possible!"

That predictable reaction made it harder for Evelyne to continue delivering the message she had been sent to transmit to her daughter. "My daughter, please understand that Letivi is and will always be your son, but he is also a precious treasure for the entire community. He is the son of Bobo and his destiny calls him to lead, just as you were called to replace Mama Atiwono."

Celestine began to choke up and tears welled up in her eyes when the reality hit her about her son being for everyone and not just for her. She was at a loss for words and could only listen to her mother as she finished what she had come to say that day.

"Listen well, my daughter. What I am about to tell you must always remain our secret and you must collaborate with us to make the chiefs' plan work."

Evelyne cleared her voice and found more courage to say dryly, "Your son will be claimed by Chief Yofu as his son. He will announce soon to everyone that your son is the product of a relationship he had with an almost white woman he knew in the capital."

Celestine was so deeply shocked by those words that she was less able to speak than before. All she could utter was, "How can this be?"

Her mother tried to soothe her by stroking her back and speaking softly in a loving tone. "It is all for the best, my daughter. In time we will see the wisdom of doing things in this way. Your son must become chief and we must do everything in our power to make it so. Also, keep in mind that he is not completely devoid of royal blood, as your father is Chief Yofu's cousin.

"Do not forget my daughter that the people must never know that Bobo is the father of your son. He will become a powerful and much respected chief, but he must not become a child of a spirit god. He is a natural born leader and he shall be a great chief for our people. It will be Letivi's choice to reveal, at a time he deems appropriate, who his real father is. For now, the people will know Chief Yofu as his earthly father and it will be our secret that the spirit Bobo is his true father."

The heaviness of what Evelyne had said made it hard for Celestine to speak. After a long silence, Celestine looked into her mother's eyes and quietly uttered, "I understand. Let it be done as you have said."

Evelyne held her daughter's hand and told her, "That is all I have to say except for a few final words. Someday soon I will come to fetch Letivi and take him to your father who will take little-used back paths behind the mountain and circle back to Ataku, pretending that he came from the capital with Chief Yofu's son. The chiefs will invite all the people to meet the chosen successor of Chief Yofu. Do not be afraid my daughter. All will turn out for the best."

Evelyne stood up to bid her daughter farewell. Celestine yelled, "Letivi, your grandmother is leaving."

Letivi came running with something in his hands. Excitedly he said, "Grandma, see what I have made for you." In his hands, was an intricate woven circular placemat made of a variety of plant vines and leaves.

Evelyne was very impressed with her gift and asked, "Letivi, how did you learn to make such a wonderful thing?"

Letivi happily replied, "The plants told me how to do it. They also want you to have it."

Evelyne was almost in tears due to the wellspring of happiness that was surging within her. Her happiness was due mostly to the brilliant potential she saw in her very bright and capable grandson. She said a soft prayer to the superior God, asking Him, "Please give me many years so I can see my grandson on the chief's stool."

Some weeks passed and Celestine tried to prepare herself for the loss of her son. She explained everything to her son, but he kept saying to her, "Mother, you do not need to explain anything. I understand what my destiny as a moonchild and the son of Bobo is to be. The time has come for me, even at my very young age, to follow fully my destiny. I am ready."

Celestine was struck by the high maturity of her five-year-old son and how he could reason and talk as if he were a very wise adult. She had her own destiny to deal with and her son had his very different destiny. They both had to go their own ways and make the best of their individual fates.

The day came when Evelyne arrived to fetch Letivi. Celestine had been preparing herself for that moment, but she could not control herself and began weeping profusely. Letivi tried to console her. "Mama, don't cry. I will be all right. It is all for the best. I must do what I have been called to do. I will come to see you as often as I can. I will always love you and carry you in my heart no matter what."

Letivi gave his mother a big and lengthy hug before taking his grandmother's hand to depart into a world he had never seen. His grandmother carried on her head a small bundle wrapped in an old cloth that contained Letivi's clothes and a few belongings, including leaves and stems from all the plants in the compound. Before leaving, Letivi called loudly, "Farewell all my friends in the plant and tree world. Thank you for all you have taught me and done to help me grow up so very well. We will meet again."

As he stepped outside the boundaries of his mother's compound, he yelled to the skies, "My father, Bobo, as you can see, I am going into the world to honor you. I know you will always be with me. Thank you for being my father and for guiding me with your spirit. We are forever joined by the moon."

After about two hundred yards down the path, Chief Gyasi was waiting for his wife and grandson. He would take Letivi around the backside of the mountain and join the main highway coming from the capital. They would board a passing truck there and arrive near the village, as if coming from the capital city. Gyasi carefully explained everything to his grandson, being careful to note why they were going such a long way to get to Ataku.

Letivi stopped his grandfather, "Grandpa, you do not have to talk so much. I know we are to pretend that we came from the capital and that I will be presented as Chief Yofu's son. I know this is the way it has to be, and I am happy doing things like this. Please don't worry. All will be just fine."

Gyasi was astounded by the adult way his little grandson spoke. He told himself that Letivi was truly intelligent and wise beyond his years. He would be a great chief indeed!

Everything went as planned. When Chief Gyasi walked into the village carrying Letivi on his back, the word spread like wildfire that he was arriving with a white boy who could be none other than Chief Yofu's son from the capital city. A large crowd gathered around Gyasi and Letivi as they made their way to Chief Yofu's compound. Letivi smiled at everyone and looked deeply into their eyes. Somehow Letivi's simple regard had a calming effect on people, making them feel very much at home with the white child. They knew as soon as they laid their eyes on Letivi that he was a very special child. They thanked the gods for sending them a true gift from heaven.

Chief Yofu stood in front of the entrance to his compound once alerted to the arrival of Letivi and waited to receive his "son" and successor. Yofu could not hide his excitement. He trembled with joy when he first caught sight of Letivi. He could not wait to take Letivi into his arms and present him to the large crowd that was assembling in front of his compound.

Before Chief Gyasi could say anything to Chief Yofu, Letivi demanded to be put down. As soon as Letivi's feet hit the ground he ran the short distance separating him from Chief Yofu and jumped into his arms. As he ran, he yelled loudly, "Papa, Papa," repeatedly.

When in Chief Yofu's arms, he hugged him tightly and then turned to announce, "I am Letivi, child of the moon, son of your Chief Yofu." All present were impressed with the initiative of the little white child dressed in khaki primary school clothes who spoke with the authority of a grown man. Perhaps the most impressed was Chief Yofu, as he could not have imagined Letivi acting in such a brilliant and striking manner. The crowd lost no time in loudly applauding and singing the praises of Letivi.

Chief Yofu could think of nothing better to do than raise Letivi in his arms and say to the crowd, "People of Ataku. I present to you my son, Letivi, your future chief, the gods and ancestors willing."

Letivi raised both his hands to greet all the people who were hysterically applauding him and singing endless praises of their future white chief. Everyone began to dance in circles, inventing a song of praise that consisted of repeating with heavy beats the words, "white chief." Upon seeing and hearing Letivi, there was not any doubt in anyone's mind that he was the one who would lead their village on to bigger and better things.

People continued to rejoice into the night. Every compound was the scene of partying, singing, and dancing in thanksgiving for Letivi. The people believed that with a white chief, who was a moonchild as well, they could not do any better. Everyone agreed the destiny of the village was in very good hands. People were bursting with pride and happiness over their good fortune of having a white chief given to them. Nothing brought happiness more than knowing their fate was guaranteed to be exceptionally good.

CHAPTER SEVENTEEN
MADMAN

I t was common knowledge that the baobab always expelled what it swallowed. How quickly and where it spewed out what it consumed was unknown, but sooner or later, somewhere in the world, out came what it gobbled up. Many in the villages of Ataku and Aniko thought that after the old baobab transformed Bobovovi into a spirit it would eject his worldly body into some nearby field. The years passed, but Bobo's human form was never found. Bobo's total disappearance for such a long period led the people to believe his case was an exception to the rule. That growing belief was reinforced by the villages' top fetish priests who agreed Bobo's conversion into a spirit was done so completely that nothing was left of him for the old baobab to return to Earth.

That prevalent belief made it harder for Evelyne to keep her faith in the return of Bobo. She continued to give offerings to the old baobab and to pray to the ancient tree to return Bobo to her daughter and his son. She begged the old baobab to work with the moon to bring Bobo back on a moonbeam as he had once ridden down from Mount Ataku. Every full moon Evelyne would offer the old baobab a special offering of yam fufu and orange palm oil, pleading with all her might for the tree to work magic with the moon and return Bobo to Earth. For years she had been making her plea and praying for the return of Bobo, but she never saw a single sign of any kind that Bobo would return.

Many years ago, some months after Bobo had been consumed by the ancient baobab tree, a Whiteman in pitiful condition was found wandering in an isolated area of the tall savannah bush fifty miles away from where the old baobab stood. An *agouti* (cane rat) hunter who first spied him early one morning was so frightened by what he saw that he ran quickly to his small village located a few miles away. He recounted what he saw in the bush and returned with his village chief and a small group of men to the spot where he had observed a crazed Whiteman, ranting and raving, as he ran madly about the bush.

At first they could not see anything, but they heard in the distance some weird noises and they went cautiously in the direction from where the odd sounds were coming. They crept slowly through the high, dry grass, and when they approached the sounds, they could see a Whiteman dancing in only his underwear and gobbling like a turkey. They could see the Whiteman had been badly burnt by the sun. Bug bites and thorn cuts covered his entire body. His bare feet were blistered and bleeding. Somehow he had survived alone in the bush, without proper food or water, in that terrible condition for days or weeks.

They could see it was urgent to take the Whiteman for medical attention at the nearest health clinic. They approached the Whiteman carefully, signaling to him to follow them. When the Whiteman saw them he ran in the opposite direction, yelping like a wounded animal. The group of men pursued him through the tall elephant grass, but soon lost track of him. They ceased their pursuit of the Whiteman, saying, "Even if we catch up to him, how will we bring him under our control and take him with us?"

They decided to walk the several miles to the nearest government police station to tell them about the almost naked Whiteman running around in the bush. Walking at a brisk pace, they arrived within a couple hours at the police station. Their chief breathlessly told the three policemen what they had seen. The policemen made them repeat more slowly their incredible story, interrupting many times to ask questions. The head policeman said, "Listen, we need to inform our superior of this unbelievable tale. He will be arriving later in the day. We ask that you come back tomorrow morning ready to take us to where you saw the Whiteman."

The village chief replied, "We will return right after sunup, prepared with the ropes and nets that we will need to capture this wild Whiteman."

The men walked slowly to their village, discussing among themselves the best means for subduing the beastly Whiteman. The chief listened to their banter on the subject and finally interjected, "This is how it should be done. We will need to split into two groups. One group will chase the Whiteman toward the other group, which will have a large fishing net to throw over the Whiteman. When the Whiteman is down, we will all pounce on him with ropes, tie his hands together, and attach his feet with a short length of rope that will allow him to walk slowly, but not run."

All the men assented their agreement to the plan with loud affirmative grunts and a big, "A, ha!"

The men returned to their village and delighted all with their recounting and reenactment of their bizarre encounter with the ferocious Whiteman in the deep bush. That was the most exciting event in the village's history. No matter how many times the men told their story, the villagers would ask for them to tell it again.

They spoke until exhausted, falling asleep on the ground where they sat with visions in their heads of a maniac Whiteman stomping through the bush.

With the crowing of the first rooster, the chief and his men assembled with their nets and ropes. They marched rapidly toward the rural police station. They found four policemen waiting for them. Three policemen would go with them and one would stay behind. The policemen would take the one rifle they possessed and all their ammunition, five bullets, just in case. The chief explained their plan for capturing the Whiteman. The policemen agreed it was a good plan, but they first needed to see the Whiteman for themselves.

While the sun's rays were barely above the top of the savannah grass, they marched quickly along a dusty path that headed toward where they saw Whiteman the day before. They arrived in the area and carefully searched in all directions for any sign that would lead them to the Whiteman. They looked everywhere for over an hour and could not find any sign of the Whiteman. The policemen were beginning to doubt what the villagers told them and were talking about returning to their station. Suddenly, they heard a loud crashing sound. The noise was like a huge tree falling to the ground. The men all stood very still and listened intently for any more noise. In their heads was only one question: "What could possibly make such a loud sound?"

They did not hear anything more after that big sound. They continued preparing to investigate the origin of the sound when they heard the savannah grass near them breaking as if an elephant was charging through it. That was a frightening sound and the men were preparing to run for their lives, but they hesitated because they did not know in which direction to run. The head policeman was very spooked and yelled loudly, "Let's run back the way we came!"

At that moment, the savannah grass parted in front of them and the savage Whiteman jumped out and ran by all the men, knocking two down as he crashed hard into them. As quickly as he had appeared, the Whiteman disappeared again into the tall and endless grassland. The men were in a state of shock and at a loss as to what to do next. They slowly recovered their courage and the head policeman said, "We need to be ready for the next time we hear the Whiteman get near us. Those men with nets must wait on the side of the path and we will try to get the Whiteman to chase us down the path to a point where you can throw your nets on him. I am not sure how this will work, but we need to do something to try to attract the Whiteman to come back here."

The men with the nets positioned themselves while the other men gathered at a spot in the path and began making loud noises, hoping they would attract the Whiteman back to them. More noise was heard in the bush. The men stopped making noise and listened for any sounds coming from the bush. There were the same unusual noises they had heard before. It sounded like the Whiteman was running around in circles in the tall grass. The clamor became increasingly close and the men began thinking the Whiteman would pop out of the bush at the same point he did before. Lacking a better plan, the men with the nets stood at the ready at the spot where the Whiteman had previously exited from the tall grass.

They could hear the noises getting closer. Their growing fear made a knot form in their stomachs. All of a sudden, the Whiteman again stunned everyone and leaped onto the path from the bush. The men threw their nets. The first net barely missed. The second net found its unruly target and the Whiteman fell hard to the ground, growling and rolling around in agony. The Whiteman struggled to remove the net, which had wrapped tightly around him, but the men with ropes quickly pinned him down. A hole was cut in the net so his hands could be tied. The same was done so a rope could be attached to his ankles. The Whiteman continued to grimace, grunt, and roll around frantically as he tried to free himself. It was a terrible thing for the men to see. They could not help but feel sympathy for the ensnared Whiteman.

They had captured the fearsome Whiteman, but they did not know how they would make him walk back to the station. They allowed the Whiteman to thrash about so he would become tired and still. They grabbed the Whiteman on both sides and lifted him to his feet. Although they did not like doing such a cruel thing, they tied a rope around his neck to lead him. His wild actions obliged them to maintain the fishing net wrapped around him. The Whiteman refused to budge. They pulled forcefully on the rope around his neck, but he would not move ahead. A small tree was cut down so they could use it to prod him from behind. The Whiteman still would not move an inch. In desperation, one policeman removed his thick leather belt and asked God for his pardon before firmly whacking the Whiteman on his buttocks. One whack from the belt and the Whiteman began stepping forward to the extent that the rope tied to his ankles allowed. The men were amazed that the Whiteman had not only survived, but he'd also remained very strong and defiant.

They toddled along the footpath at a very slow speed. It took them several hours to arrive at the police station. They were still very far from the health center that could treat the Whiteman tied tightly to a shady neem tree and allowed to sit down. He was given a bowl of water and corn mush. The net was cut away from his face so he could drink and eat. He quickly devoured his food and water, and more of the same was brought to him. There seemed to be no limit to how much the famished and dehydrated Whiteman could eat and drink. After many servings, the Whiteman fell into a deep slumber, snoring so loudly the ground around him vibrated.

The head policeman decided the only way they could take him to the health center was in a vehicle. He, therefore, decided to walk the five miles to the nearest district administrative post to provide a full report and to send a telegram to his superiors in the capital city about the entire bizarre incident. He told the men, "Please stay here until I return. I will try to come back tomorrow with the chief administrator's vehicle and take the Whiteman to the health center. I will send a full report and ask for advice on what to do with the Whiteman. Do not disturb the Whiteman. Let him sleep."

The Whiteman slept the rest of that day and the entire night, and was still sleeping when the policeman returned late in the morning the next day with the head administrator in a rickety old Peugeot pickup truck. They were happy the Whiteman was still in a deep sleep, but his labored breathing made them fear he was ill. They parked the pickup near the Whiteman. The rope was detached from the tree trunk and the men lifted him into the pickup bed. The Whiteman remained asleep as the pickup whisked him off to medical attention at the district health center.

When they arrived at the health center, the Whiteman was still asleep in spite of the bumpy road and the uncomfortable corrugated metal floor of the pickup bed. People gathered around to stare at the sleeping Whiteman in the fishing net tied up like a wild beast. They took the Whiteman into the rustic rural clinic and placed him on a flimsy metal-frame bed with a worn foam mattress. Two nurses immediately injected him in both arms with heavy doses of penicillin and hooked him to an intravenous drip from a large bottle filled with saline solution, antibiotics, and vitamins. His many wounds and scratches were treated with an antiseptic and the worst sores were bandaged. The Whiteman remained asleep and snored so loudly he disturbed the other patients.

The receipt of the telegram by various government offices in the capital city of Melomti caused quite a stir. The president and his top advisors were informed. The main question on everybody's minds was, "Who is this Whiteman?"

The minister of foreign affairs sent an official correspondence to all the western embassies, inquiring if any of their nationals were missing. Each embassy reviewed its files and made queries, but as far as they could tell, none of their nationals were missing. The negative reports from the embassies prompted the government to begin referring to the man discovered in the distant bush as the "White Mystery." They decided to send someone from their national security office to take the White Mystery's fingerprints. Their intention was to provide the fingerprints to Interpol to check against their voluminous files of prints.

The day after the Whiteman was taken to the clinic, he awoke. He remained perfectly still and was stone silent. He stared deeply into everyone's face with his greenish, snakelike eyes. He became peaceful enough that the fishing net and ropes were removed from him. His ankle rope remained in place. One end of a rope was tied to his leg and the other end was tied to his bed. The rope was just long enough to permit him to go to the latrine that was just outside his room. The Whiteman slept most of the time, except when he was brought food. He always ate his food rapidly and completely, throwing his tin bowl on the concrete floor when he was finished, indicating emphatically that the food given to him was never enough.

The Whiteman fully cooperated with the agents who came from the capital a couple of days later to take his prints. The dark black ink was rolled across his fingers and thumbs of both hands and his prints were taken on special white paper. The only problem encountered was when they wanted to clean his fingers with rubbing alcohol. The Whiteman refused the cleaning, preferring to rub the black ink across his body. Such an action confirmed to those observing him that he had indeed lost his mind and needed mental care.

The national security office submitted the Whiteman's fingerprints by fax to Interpol and within forty-eight hours a report came back with a positive match. According to Interpol, those were the prints of David Peterson, a US citizen from Kansas. The minister of foreign affairs immediately telephoned the American ambassador to inform him of the information received from Interpol. The ambassador quickly asked his staff to review immediately their files for any trace of a man named David Peterson.

A couple of hours later the Peace Corps director called the ambassador to tell him there had once been a volunteer with that name, but he had ended his service years ago. The Peace Corps thought he had returned to his home in the States along with all the other volunteers in his group. In any event, nobody had ever inquired about David and his whereabouts. The ambassador responded pointedly, "Evidently, he never left, as fingerprints don't lie. We need to mobilize quickly a team to bring him to the capital city so we can evacuate him to his home in the States."

The next day the embassy sent one of its largest Chevrolet Suburban utility vehicles the fifty miles upcountry to fetch the man identified as David. The embassy physician and security officer accompanied the driver. The rural clinic had been advised of their arrival on that day. Following their arrival, they quickly assessed David's situation and injected him with a strong sedative. David fell into a deep, drug-induced sleep. They cleansed him with alcohol swabs and dressed him in a hospital gown. To be on the safe side, they gently placed a straitjacket on him. They left the rope tied to his ankles in place. They placed him on the portable cot they had brought with them and carried him to the back of the Suburban. They slid the cot into the vehicle and secured it tightly to the floor with prepositioned bolts.

They thanked the clinic staff and zoomed back to the capital. They strapped David into a bed in the embassy's tiny clinic and rotated staff so he would be watched around the clock. They administered a full physical checkup and found David fit to travel. In the meantime, the embassy's consular section was working feverishly to identify David's next of kin. It appeared that David was almost an orphan, had very few relatives, and never had been in contact with anyone in the United States. After much searching, they located a much older brother, Edgar, living in Gemini, Kansas, who was willing to take in a brother he had not had any contact with for many years. Edgar took the money he had been saving for his old age and used it to buy David an airline ticket home. A photo was taken of David and his new US passport was quickly made, using the information that was found in his old Peace Corps records. The embassy physician would accompany David on his flight home, keeping him well sedated. The embassy and the physician also wrote up a full report to share with local authorities in Kansas once David was home.

Their flights to Kansas were uneventful. David was never fully conscious because of the heavy sedation. He was kept fully restrained. At the two airports where they had to change flights, David was buckled into a wheelchair and whisked ahead of all the other passengers to his plane. Local officials in Kansas had been advised of David's arrival at the closest airport to Gemini and were waiting for him and the embassy physician. The embassy's physician handed David and his papers over to the officials. He said, "I really do not know what happened to him or what is wrong with him. It looks like he had some kind of severe culture shock and became mentally unstable. He needs close evaluation and proper psychiatric treatment. Everything is written up in the documents contained in the envelopes I just gave you. I am sorry, but I have to catch my flight back to Africa."

The officials thanked the physician heartily for bringing David home. He was assured that David would get the best of care. They wheeled David to a waiting ambulance and took him to the nearest state mental hospital often referred to as "Third Hill," because it was located on the third hill outside the city limits of a town located not far from Gemini. Hospital staff were waiting for David and quickly admitted him. Although they found nothing wrong with David, and he was completely peaceful and harmless, they kept him for two years before releasing him to his brother Edgar and his wife, Beatrice. David lived with them in their modest home in Gemini. By then he had developed such a large potbelly that the neighborhood children gave him the name Jelly Belly, or simply J.B.

Nobody could have guessed then that J.B. would become a great inspiration to his neighbors and a local folklore hero. J.B.'s neighbors did not know he had been in Africa and they had no knowledge of what happened to him while he was there. They could not know or even imagine that his destiny was still in Africa. All they saw was an odd, short, rotund man taking his daily walks in the neighborhood and acting in a strange way that endeared him to them, making them want to improve their lives. J.B. unintentionally had a powerful effect on all those he came in contact with, but really all J.B.'s inner soul was yearning for was to return to the old baobab tree in Africa that had swallowed him and spat him out.

CHAPTER EIGHTEEN
STAR PUPIL

Letivi was an exceptional standout at his elite Catholic boys boarding school located just outside the capital city of Melomti. His comparatively light complexion made him easy to spot, but it was his intellectual prowess and profound wisdom that most impressed his Jesuit teachers and fellow students. He made schoolwork look easy. It was as if he already had all the answers. He was miles ahead of everyone in every subject. Genius was not an adequate enough term to describe Letivi's abundant natural gifts.

Students and teachers alike sought out Letivi for advice, counsel, and information. If Letivi did not have the answers they sought, he would tell them to give him time to think about it and come back to see him in a few days. Letivi would search his mind and the school's library for the answers. He devoured anything he read and never forgot a word. His ability to speed-read and his photographic memory enabled him to read every book in the school library, even the dictionaries and encyclopedias. He was given permission on weekends to peruse the books at the national university library and the state archives.

His hunger for knowledge could not be satisfied and he was always looking for more sources of information. He sought and engaged all the intellectuals in the country. As his reputation grew and he became older, people from all walks of life sought to engage him in a dialogue. Such dialogues became large school assemblies for all to attend. Everyone benefited from Letivi's immense gifts. By associating with Letivi, other students lifted their own academic performance and the school became known for having the best results on the annual national exams. In many ways, Letivi was helping mold a number of future leaders of the country.

In his spare time, Letivi amused himself by learning Greek and Latin from the foreign priests who managed his school. By the age of ten, Letivi spoke those languages so fluently the priests called him "Mousaios," the only mortal son of the Greek moon goddess, Selene. Letivi also mastered French, the main national language and the language of instruction at his school, as well as English. Letivi found learning languages was lots of fun for him and allowed him to read books in those languages.

Letivi loved attending mass daily at school and learning all he could about the Bible and its contents. He enjoyed engaging the priests in discussions about Christian doctrine. By the time he was in high school, the priests at his school were convinced he possessed all the qualities desired of a high-performing leader of the Catholic Church. They were convinced he should transfer to a special seminary school in the Vatican. When that ideal opportunity was raised with Letivi, he immediately and emphatically rejected it, "Going to the Vatican would take me farther away from my destiny instead of closer to it. I must finish my studies here and return to my village to do my father's business. This is the only way for me."

The priests were perturbed by the reply. They saw in Letivi a great talent that should be shared with the world and not lost in some poor African village. They deployed many efforts to change Letivi's mind. They informed the Vatican. Three Italian bishops came from Rome to meet Letivi and persuade him to study in the Vatican. Letivi's consistent refusal to budge from his hard and fast position caused them to travel to Ataku to talk with the aging Chief Yofu and Chief Gyasi, pleading with them to intervene and make Letivi go to seminary in the Vatican. They responded, "Letivi is the master of his own destiny and it is fully up to him to decide what he will do. We recognize his many talents and we will support him in anything he chooses to do."

The bishops asked for their support in inviting Letivi to the Vatican for a visit during the next school break. The chiefs again said, "Letivi knows his life's path and what he has been called to do on Earth. Only he can decide if he wants to visit the Vatican or not. Ask him, not us!"

The chiefs thanked the bishops for honoring them and their village by their visit. "We are truly blessed by your presence among us and we are very thankful for all the interest you have shown in our precious Letivi. We know he has great promise, but only he knows what he has to do. We ask before you go that you bless this village and its population, which has assembled in great numbers to greet you and receive your blessing."

The bishops were stunned when they stepped out of Chief Yofu's compound. As far as their eyes could see, an unending crowd of people had amassed. There was a great river of people flowing down the mountain slope and overflowing into byways and the road below. People had come running from the entire region to receive their first ever "Vatican blessing." The bishops were overwhelmed. They thought they had come for a simple visit with village chiefs, but they were confronted with a potential religious revival of large proportions. They had never encountered such a situation, and they were fully unprepared to administer to the masses. They could speak, but how could they give the people the blessing they sought without holy water? Moreover, they were not dressed for such an auspicious occasion.

The head bishop, Xavier, told his two companions they would have to find some water and pray over it so it could be sanctified and used to sprinkle on the people. Xavier spoke in an urgent tone, "You two stay here and lead the crowd in saying Hail Mary's while I return to ask for the chief's help in assembling buckets of clean water that I can bless."

Bishop Xavier quickly told the chiefs that he needed several buckets of water. The chiefs in turn told the women and children in the compound to bring to the bishop as much water as they could. Many galvanized buckets, clay pots, and calabashes full of clear water were gathered and brought to Bishop Xavier, who immediately began administering the sacraments required to make the water holy and fit for blessing the people.

The bishop asked the women to bring all their short straw brooms. He told them that he and his brother bishops would need those to dip into the water and cast droplets of holy water on the people as they administered Christ's almighty's blessing on the assembled. The brooms were quickly brought to the bishop and he selected three from among them. He asked the chiefs to allow the women to follow him with the water containers. Chief Yofu turned to the women, "You have been chosen by the bishop to accompany these men of the cross as they bless the crowd with this holy water. Consider yourselves as blessed."

As the women picked up the water containers, Yofu remained seated in his chief's chair and asked Bishop Xavier, "Holy Father. I beg you to bless this compound and all the people in it before you go into the crowd."

Bishop Xavier gently responded and dipped one of the brooms he was holding in the nearest bucket of water and gave the church's holy blessing to the chiefs and everyone in the compound. As soon as the bishop dipped the broom in the water, all the people in the compound, except the aged Chief Yofu, fell to their knees to receive the blessing. They remained kneeling for as long as they could to allow for the full goodness of the Godly blessing to penetrate deeply into their souls.

When Bishop Xavier exited the chief's compound, the masses knelt with their heads bowed as his two companions continuously made the sign of the cross and said Hail Mary's repeatedly as loud as they could in Latin. "Hail Mary, full of grace. The Lord is with thee. Blessed are thou among women, and blessed is the fruit of thy womb, Jesus. Holy Mary, Mother of God, pray for us sinners, now and at the hour of our death. Amen."

The people did not understand what was being said and most were not Catholic, but they strongly felt the spirit of God at work and many among them became overwhelmed by the force of the Holy Spirit. That powerful force worked to interconnect everyone who was open to receive it. Chiefs Yofu and Gyasi were deeply affected by what they saw and felt. Standing near them was the high fetish priest, Kontor, and he whispered to them, "My chiefs, this is the strongest spiritual tide I have ever witnessed in all my long years. Our grandfathers and African gods and spirits have happily joined with this Catholic ceremony to cause a spiritual tidal wave never seen before by any of us. We must prepare ourselves for a genuine spiritual reawakening of major proportions."

Bishop Xavier joined his brethren and held high the golden cross hanging from his necklace with his left hand while holding as high as he could his right hand showing the peace sign. With the making of that sign, the two other junior bishops ceased their litany of Hail Mary's. Bishop Xavier stood quietly for a few minutes as he asked the Lord to give him the strength he needed to do His work on Earth at that moment. During those few minutes, all was exceedingly quiet. No one made a sound, neither the babies nor animals, nor any living thing. The only sound was from a distant evil crow, which was fleeing far away as fast as possible from the spiritual upheaval.

Feeling the power of God within him, Bishop Xavier began by reciting in Latin "Our Father."

"Our Father, who art in heaven, hallowed be thy name. Thy Kingdom come; thy will be done on Earth as it is in heaven. Give us this day our daily bread; and forgive us our trespasses as we forgive those who trespass against us; and lead us not in temptation but deliver us from evil. Amen."

As those words flowed from Bishop Xavier's mouth, a strong spiritual wave rolled through the crowd and many were emotionally overcome by the Holy Spirit, falling prostrate to the ground as if possessed. They trembled slightly and tears flowed profusely from their eyes. People braced themselves to confront the full force of the Holy Spirit. Nobody could know who would be next to succumb to the mighty power of God.

The bishops were awed by what was happening and they feared they would not be able to leave the village as planned. They, too, could feel the Holy Spirit at work in a way they had never experienced before. They knew they must trust and obey God and do His bidding. Bishop Xavier knew the sprinkling of holy water on the people would add fuel to the spiritual revival already occurring, but he had no choice. He began walking through the crowds with his brethren and the women at their sides carrying holy water.

The bishops walked through the crowd, stopping every few yards to provide a blessing to those around them. They dipped the short brooms into the water and flicked into the air droplets of water so that everyone around would have some holy water drops fall on them. When many people felt the drops touch them they fell to the ground, crying loudly their thanks to God. The bishops kept making the sign of the cross and repeating in unison:

"God our father, your gift of water brings life and freshness to the earth, washes away our sins, and brings eternal life. We ask you now to bless this water and to give us the protection on this day, which you have made your own. Renew the living spring of your life within us and protect us in spirit and body so that we may be free from sin and come into your presence to receive your gift of salvation. We ask this through Christ our Lord. Amen."

It took the bishops over two hours to sprinkle holy water on all the people. Mothers approached the bishops with their babies, pleading with them to place their hands on the babies and make the sign of the cross on their foreheads with their thumbs. Everyone wanted to receive the maximum possible spiritual benefit from that unique religious occasion. They knew they would never again have three bishops from the Vatican among them. The receiving of babies took a long time and the bishops needed to be on their way before dark. They approached their car and bid a final farewell to the crowd, slowly making a last sign of the cross and saying softly a prayer to God to bless the people and their village.

The bishops departed, but it took much longer for the heavy presence of the Holy Spirit to lift from the hearts of the villagers. All those exposed to the spiritual event were touched for life, and they would thank God forever for bringing the bishops to them. The chiefs reminded the people that the bishops came because of how highly they regarded Letivi, their future chief. Chief Yofu issued a proclamation that was read in every household. "We thank God almighty for the huge blessing the bishops brought to us, but we thank even more our chief-to-be, Letivi, for being the kind of person for whom bishops from the Vatican would travel so far to see. We are very fortunate indeed to have Letivi. He is truly God's gift to us. Let us all thank God for Letivi and what he has already done for us. We shall never forget the blessing he gave us this day. I am sure he will bring us many more blessings."

On the ride back to Melomti, the bishops sank into deep reflection. They were trying to digest the profound spiritual movement they had experienced in Ataku. They could see that Ataku was a very special place and they understood better how a simple village could produce such a superstar as Letivi. It made them want even more for Letivi to come to the Vatican for training for positions of great responsibility within the church, which needed men with Letivi's intelligence and many talents. For them, Letivi was also a gift from God that needed to be shared more widely and not just with one village in Africa.

The bishops met with Letivi and his headmaster again. Letivi had already heard about what happened when they went to his village and he thanked them for bringing such a bountiful blessing to Ataku. They spoke for hours. The bishops tried every way they knew to persuade Letivi to come with them to the Vatican for a special program of education. Letivi was adamant. He said repeatedly and most firmly, "I cannot leave my country because I do not know when my father will die and return. I cannot deviate from my destiny."

The bishops were confused by the repeated phrase. They understood he was to replace his father, Chief Yofu, when he died, but they did not know what he meant when he said "return." They did not know he was cryptically referring to his biological father, Bobovovi, who Letivi knew in his innermost self would return some day. He could not be far away when that day happened. The bishops finally had to leave, but before leaving they said unambiguously. "Letivi, we leave you with our blessing. We give you our highest respect. We ask that you never forget you have a place in the Vatican anytime you wish to occupy it. Good-bye, our precious Letivi, we pray we will see you with us someday."

In the days that followed, Letivi continued with his high school work. His popularity grew. He was not only popular at his school, but he had a highly regarded reputation across the entire country. He was often invited to national events as a speaker, and he was a lecturer at the university. Everyone was impressed by Letivi and happy to have a light-skinned person among them. It was for most people a blessing to have one of their own add diversity to a homogenous black population. It was good to have a "White" who spoke their language and possessed the same mannerisms and gestures. More than anything, it was good to have a man like Letivi who knew them and the many challenges they faced in life.

Letivi kept in close touch with Ataku. Every time anyone would come from the village they would pass by Letivi's school to see him. Letivi always gave of his time and himself for anyone from the village. Chief Gyasi visited his grandson once a month and brought him all the village news and messages from his mother. Each time Chief Gyasi returned to Ataku, he held a meeting with clan heads and elders to report on how Letivi was doing. That constant communication on the impressive performance of Letivi helped forge a strong bind between Letivi and the village. Moreover, it made the people increasingly happy they would one day have a chief of very high caliber.

Every school holiday Letivi visited Ataku. He would always find a way to sneak through the forest to see his mother and say hello to his plant and tree friends. Those were always joyous occasions. In each of those visits, Chiefs Yofu and Gyasi, and senior elders, would provide Letivi instruction on the duties and responsibilities of being a chief. They did all they could to prepare Letivi for the chieftaincy. Their work was lessened by the keen intelligence and intuition of Letivi, who appeared many times to know as much, if not more, as they did. Letivi could not tell them the plants and trees had taught him many things. His ability to communicate with indigenous plants and trees had to be kept a secret.

Letivi was disappointed that the plants and trees at his school would not talk to him. He began to think they could not talk. He asked his mother why that was so and she explained, "My dear son, it is only those plants and trees that are in their original home that can talk. Once they have been taken away and replanted elsewhere they lose their ability to talk. This is one reason why I have been called to preserve this old place in the forest. My job is to ensure our knowledge of plants will not be lost and the knowledge that plants can give us will remain with us. As chief, you must work to always preserve this place. It is the last of its kind."

Letivi could hear in the wind under a full moon night that his time to become chief was nearing. That made him sad, as he knew it meant Chief Yofu was approaching the end of his time on Earth. Chief Yofu had lived much longer than he had expected. In the past few years, he had spent much of his time lying down or in his easy chair. He slept most of the time. He was often in a silent conversation with the ancestors who were preparing to receive him among them. For several years, he had one foot in this world and one foot in the other world that awaited everyone after death. At a moment least expected, Chief Yofu went to sleep and quietly put both feet in the other world. His last words to the grandfathers were, "I am ready now. I have been blessed by three bishops from the Vatican. I am now at peace. I am coming now to join you."

CHAPTER NINETEEN
LAST RITES

It was hard for the people of Ataku to respect Chief Yofu's instructions and break with tradition by offering him a simple funeral. For generations their chiefs had been honored with lavish funeral ceremonies that cost the village dearly. Chief Yofu had been sitting on the royal stool for over forty years and deserved all the funeral honors reserved for the most extraordinary of chiefs. Tradition called for a week of feasting and many extravagant ceremonies.

Chief Yofu had instructed before his death that there was not to be any such ostentatious funeral for him. He said those were negative traditional practices that a poor village had no business doing. For Chief Yofu, it was time to change and stop the wasteful practice of overspending on funerals. It would be better to invest money spent for funerals on more productive investments like the education of children. He said the same thing about marriages and baptisms. He urged that the practice of bride-price payments be banned. He made it clear before his death that his funeral should be as simple and cheap as possible.

Unhappy carpenters built a plain, unvarnished, roughly hewn wood coffin for Chief Yofu from the cheapest of woods. They were unhappy because in the past they would make good money by building fancy coffins for important dignitaries. They made little money making Chief Yofu's barebox coffin. That simple coffin was placed on an old table in the thatch-covered rotunda meeting hangar within the chief's compound. Chairs were placed around the coffin for elders and family members. At one end were two chief's chairs for Chief Gyasi and Letivi.

Before Chief Yofu's body was placed in the coffin for viewing by the villagers, senior elders gathered to remove, in secret, some of his hair, fingernails, and tiny pieces of his flesh. Those body parts would be wrapped in a cloth that had been prayed over by the chief fetish priest, Kontor, and put in a small wooden box. After elaborate secret ceremonies conducted by Kontor at night, that box would be placed in a designated spot within the grandfathers' house reserved for chiefs. In that way, parts of Chief Yofu would join his predecessors and he would maintain his link with the earthly world.

As he had instructed, the elders dressed Chief Yofu's body in his everyday clothes. His more expensive royal garments would be saved for his successor. Kerosene lamps were placed around his coffin along the edges of the table and hung from the rafters above him. Elders and family members were seated on benches and chairs arranged along the outer circumference. Chief Gyasi and Letivi sat at the head of the casket. The eerie shadows cast by the flickering lamps gave the solemn event a supernatural air.

Chief Gyasi and Letivi circled the coffin first. Each mumbled softly some words that meant, "Good-bye, our chief. Hello, our eternal grandfather."

They were followed in order of seniority by the elders and family members. When the group had finished saying their last words to their defunct leader and family patriarch, villagers started streaming into the compound, passing quietly in a single file procession in front of their dead chief. The members of the oldest clan passed first, followed by the next oldest clan, and so forth. It took several hours for every man, woman, and child to pay their last respects to their dearly departed Chief Yofu.

Chief Gyasi, Letivi, and senior elders would remain with the corpse all night. Just before dawn they would secretly carry the body away to a burial place only known to them. It was the tradition that chiefs were buried in secret to prevent any enemies from finding the body. Nobody knew where any of the chiefs were buried. Each chief was buried secretly in a different place chosen by the head fetish priest. Letivi's grandfather, Chief Gyasi, told him about those customs, as he participated in the burial of his surrogate father. His participation in the chief's funeral was an important part of his preparation for ultimately replacing Chief Yofu.

By daylight the next morning, Chief Yofu was gone. Tradition demanded that nobody talk about the chief's death. If anyone asked about the chief, people would respond in a deceptive manner. They would usually say, "He has traveled to the capital city." No outsiders should know their chief had passed on to the other world until a new chief was sitting on the royal stool. The aim was to make it appear to the outside world that all was well and Chief Yofu was fine. Of course, it was often hard to hide the truth about the passing of a chief, particularly one as prominent as Chief Yofu.

The same morning Chief Yofu's mortal remains were scurried secretly away, his numerous wives and elder children picked up some old clay pots in their compound that had been used by the chief. They carried those pots on their heads to the field of broken pots located just outside the village. It was a sacred place covered by thousands of pottery shards. They looked for a spot where there were not many shards. After a brief prayer, they raised the pots over their heads and slammed them to the ground as hard as they could. The pots shattered into many fragments. When they had done that, all said, "Good-bye, Yofu. Please look over us. We will see you in the next world."

The shattering of clay pots for every dead person poignantly demonstrated the belief that death was like a broken pot, as once it was broken it could not be mended. The field of broken pots was the most sacred place in the village. People were afraid to go anywhere near the field at night because they believed that was where the spirits of the dead congregated. Offerings were often left before sunset for the dead in that sacred field. Since the food was always gone the next day, there was no doubt in the people's minds that the spirits of the dead consumed it.

While Chief Yofu's family was trudging to the field of broken pots to administer his last rites, Chief Gyasi remained in Yofu's meeting room with Letivi and senior elders. They were discussing the transition to the time when Letivi would be chief. Chief Gyasi spoke in a matter-of-fact tone, "I will serve as regent until Letivi finishes his high school studies. Shortly after his high school graduation he will return home and undergo all the ceremonies required to be proclaimed chief."

The elders grunted their assent, but Letivi's mind seemed to be elsewhere. The moody Letivi despondently reacted. "Thank you, my chief. I ask for a few days to think about all this before transition plans are concluded. I need some time alone to consider what comes next in my life."

Chief Gyasi and the elders were puzzled by Letivi's words and the hesitancy with which he spoke, but they saw no harm in allowing him a few days to reflect. "Very well, our chief-to-be. Let us all think some more and meet here again in a day or two." In that manner, Chief Gyasi ended the meeting and bid farewell to all, wishing them safe return to their respective homes.

After that meeting, Letivi took some back paths to his real grandmother's house in the Aniko quarter. That was where he often stayed when he came to the village. He told his grandmother in a very serious way, "Please tell anyone who asks if I am here that I am not available. I wish to spend a day or two with your daughter, my mother, in her forest enclave. I wish to have some time alone."

Grandmother Evelyne replied in her soft, understanding voice, "I know, my grandson. Please go and stay with your mother. She will be very happy to see you." At the same time, she was thinking it odd that her grandson wanted to be alone. People growing up in communal society, like the one that prevailed in Ataku, never knew what "alone" meant, and, therefore, would feel very sad and awkward if they found themselves experiencing unaccustomed aloneness.

Letivi thanked her and added, "Grandmother, the moon will soon be full. Please do not go to the old baobab. I will go there and I need to be alone with the old tree."

Evelyne raised her eyebrows and wanted to query her grandson on the subject, but she bit her lip and said, "I know you must do what you have to do. I will not go to the old baobab as I usually do at the coming full moon. You may be able to learn what I have not been able to learn from the baobab in my full moon visits over many years."

Before she could finish her words, Letivi said good-bye and went in the opposite direction of where his mother was located. He did that to fool any onlookers. He would later go deep into the bush and circle back on seldom used paths to his mother's forest redoubt.

Long before Letivi arrived at his mother's place, the trees had already told her that he was coming. Her heart filled with joy when she heard the news that her son was on his way. She could not wait to see again the fine young man he had grown to be. There was a great clamor among the trees and plants as Letivi arrived to embrace his mother. Tears flowed down her cheeks. No words could describe the profound love Celestine felt for her son, who loved his mother just as deeply.

A mixture of emotion tormented Letivi. His mother was asking one question after another and the plant world was directing at him a cacophony of voices. Letivi finally raised his voice and said rapidly in all languages. "Please give me some quiet. I plan to stay here for two nights; therefore, we will have plenty of time to talk. Right now I want to rest and talk to my mother."

He spoke with his mother the rest of the day and well into the evening. They spoke of his experiences at school and about her life as Mama Atibona, master of the plant world. They laughed a lot and never tired of speaking to one another. They wanted to savor every ounce of their time together. When it came time to sleep, Letivi said to the plants, "Good night to all of you. We will talk the first thing tomorrow morning. I have something I need to ask you."

The plants bid him goodnight and told him they were happy he would talk to them and that he had not forgotten about them. The exhausted Letivi fell asleep immediately on the grass mat Celestine had placed for him under an old mahogany tree. Letivi's night was one filled with the same dream repeating itself. In his dream, he was at the foot of the ancient baobab waiting for his real father, Bobovovi, to return. He could hear in his dream the old baobab saying in a rough, almost unintelligible voice, "Wait here for your father. He is coming back."

When Letivi woke up the next morning, the same vision continued to whirl around in his head. He told his mother about his dream. She did not know what to say. She had desperately wished and prayed for years for Bobovovi's return. She had done all she could to bring her beloved Bobovovi back, but no signs of any kind had been revealed to her. She thought that maybe the signs she had sought would be revealed to her gifted son. "Mother, I am now convinced I must spend the night with the old baobab tonight when the moon will be full. I feel something is about to happen and I must be there. I know the old baobab wants me there."

The next morning Letivi carried on a long conversation with the plants and trees. In particular, he pressed the trees for any information they could give him on how to communicate with the old baobab. The oldest tree near his mother's compound dominated that part of the conversation and concluded by saying, "The ancient baobab is much older than any of us and the tree dialect he uses died out long ago. There may be some words in this dialect that are nearly the same, but, in general, the language he uses is unintelligible to us."

Letivi found it hard to believe that the old baobab had not learned other languages in the hundreds of years he had been on Earth. Late that afternoon he set out to see the baobab, following a series of back paths that would lead him to the open place in the tall savannah grass where the towering old baobab stood mightily and majestically. He greeted the baobab in the standard tree language and said, "I am here for the night. I expect you will tell me something about my father, Bobovovi, who you swallowed before I was born many years ago."

After saying firmly in a loud voice those heartfelt words, Letivi reclined on a grassy spot near the base of the baobab. He looked up at the giant tree towering over him. He pondered how its natural ugliness contrasted with its magnificent presence. He gazed at the tree as the fading rays of the sun filtered through its barren branches, making it look like it was on fire.

At that moment, the glowing tree somehow touched Letivi's heart and he began to feel an uncontrollable affection for the old baobab. The thought that it was the last place his father Bobovovi had been seen on the Earth added to his growing emotional state. It was indeed a tree that had been sacred since before people had settled in that land. It was believed that the tree was over a thousand years old.

For reasons he could not fathom, he stood up and walked around the large seventy-foot circumference of the tree five times. He had been told there was an opening in the tree that his father had entered to stay the night, but he never exited the tree. He could see no sign of any opening in the tree and wondered if the story he had been told many times by his mother was true or just another village fable.

Letivi returned to the spot where he had started, laid both hands on the tree, and said a prayer in tree language, "Dear Sacred Baobab. It is your servant, Letivi. I come for my father whom I have never known. I know you loved him because you took him away to the spirit world. I promise my love to you forever if you can bring my father back to me. You know my heart, and you know why I am here. I know you can help me. I am willing to do anything you ask if you bring my father back to me. Thank you, most ancient and respected one."

The brilliant scarlet sunset lingered longer than usual, but its ephemeral glory was quickly erased by the abrupt fall of a very dark night. The darkness was perforated by the light of thousands of sparkling stars spread endlessly across the heavens. The rising full moon that flooded the land with a bright white light gradually diluted the spectacular starlight and diminished greatly the difference between day and night. Letivi was in awe of the beauty of the baobab in the moonlight. The old tree was more beautiful under the light of the moon than it had been under the fading sunlight. It was as if the baobab and the full moon made a perfect couple.

Letivi settled in for a long night. As a moonchild, his inner being was stirred and soothed simultaneously by bathing in the rays of the full moon. The effect of the full moon made it so he could not shut his eyes or sit still. He turned in circles, not knowing what to do, as he tried to evenly distribute the rays of the moon on the front and back of his body. He took off his clothes so he could receive the full force of the moon's rays. He danced around the old baobab like a crazy loon, calling repeatedly, "Oh, moon! Your child welcomes you. Pour your blessing on me. Help me open the old baobab's mouth."

When the moon was directly overhead, Letivi could see the tree trembling slightly. He placed his hands on the tree to see if it were true that it was vibrating. The moment he placed his hands on the tree, it stopped vibrating and he could hear one word, "soon." He knew that word because it was the same word used in the current tree language. He was stunned that he could hear so clearly the word. At the same time, he was puzzled by what the old baobab was telling him. What did "soon" mean?

At dawn's first light, Letivi was on his way back to the village. He was not sure what "soon" meant, but he was sure that it meant he had to stay in the village to find out. He went to his grandmother's house to bathe and change clothes. His grandmother could see that he was in an agitated state and her concern prompted her to ask, "My dear Letivi child, what happened during the night with the old baobab?

Letivi was in a rush and had no time for any conversation. He quipped, "I do not know what to say except that I need to see immediately your husband, Chief Gyasi. It is urgent that we talk. There is no time to lose. Excuse me, grandmother, for my impoliteness, but I must see Chief Gyasi now. Where is he?"

"He is chairing village court in Chief Yofu's compound in Ataku. Please tell me, my son, I beg you. Did the baobab tell you anything?"

Letivi curtly answered his grandmother by saying, "Yes, he spoke to me, but he said only one word, 'soon.'" He quickly strode off, leaving his grandmother standing in an uneasy state. He walked at a brisk pace to confront his grandfather in Ataku.

His grandmother walked behind him for a short distance, begging him to tell her what the old baobab meant by "soon." Letivi was rushing and had no time to talk. He snapped, "Grandmother, I have no time. I do not know what the baobab meant! Please leave me now."

Letivi arrived out of breath at the room where Chief Gyasi was in a village council session with the elders. Letivi entered brusquely. All could easily see that something was wrong with him. The chief and elders were examining him closely when he blurted out, "Excuse me for so rudely interrupting, but I must speak now in private with Chief Gyasi. Please give us a few minutes alone. Thank you."

After the stunned elders filed silently out of the room, Letivi turned to his grandfather and simply said, "My time has come. My time is now!"

Chief Gyasi was unsure of what Letivi meant and asked him to explain himself. Letivi told him of what the old baobab had said. While his grandfather raised his eyebrows and gave him an incredulous look, Letivi quickly explained, "It is my time to become chief now. I must be chief when the baobab's 'soon' happens."

"But, my dear grandson, you need to finish high school before becoming chief. There remains at least two years before you complete your college preparatory courses and receive your diploma."

Letivi cut his grandfather off by saying, "I do not need a diploma to be a good chief. I already know more than the teachers. There is nothing more for me to learn in that school. My place is here. I will become chief now or never. It is urgent. I hear my destiny calling me."

Letivi's words left Chief Gyasi speechless. He was deeply surprised and confused by what Letivi was saying. He had been truly caught off guard and did not know what to say. He could only ask, "Are you sure? Is this your final decision?"

"Yes, I am certain that to fulfill my destiny I must now become chief. My talk with the baobab has convinced me of that!"

Chief Gyasi agonized for a few minutes, but he could see it was pointless to try to change Letivi's mind. He knew Letivi already possessed all the qualities sought in an outstanding chief and he had no doubt that he would be a great chief. He had no choice but to agree with Letivi and say, "Your wish will be done as you have so passionately requested. We will start immediately preparing you to sit on the royal stool. I will now inform the elders waiting outside."

The elders returned to the meeting room and took their seats. Chief Gyasi and Letivi stood together in front of them. Gyasi said in an authoritative voice, "I present to you your new chief, Letivi."

The elders were surprised by Chief Gyasi's words. At first they thought a practical joke was being played on them. They looked at one another with questioning faces. The senior elder asked for an explanation.

Chief Gyasi tried to elaborate. "My brothers, there have been signs indicating now is the time that Letivi must take his position as chief of our village. He will not be returning to school. We need to start preparing immediately the ceremonies required to confirm him as our chief."

The elders remained silent for several minutes until the oldest among them rose to his feet and said, "We salute you, Chief Letivi. We are honored to serve you."

The elders all applauded and shouted thanks to the gods and the ancestors. They proceeded one by one to kneel quickly before Letivi, shaking his hand and thanking him for agreeing to be their chief.

The word spread like wildfire from the chief's compound to all corners of the village and beyond. When they heard the unexpected news about Letivi remaining in the village, people stopped what they were doing, sang praises, and thanked the heavens. They had all been waiting for the day when Letivi would become chief. They were pleased and excited to learn he would sit on the royal stool sooner instead of later. It was indeed a day for rejoicing and thanking God for their good fortune. It was a great feeling to know that the benefits they thought would take years to reap would happen within weeks. It was like winning the lottery jackpot before the tickets were drawn.

CHAPTER TWENTY
CHIEF LETIVI

Letivi left the chief's compound and proceeded to visit every house in the village. He warmly greeted every family and acclaimed how happy he was to serve them as their new chief. He shook the hand of every man and woman, telling them he was glad to know them and he was determined to be a good chief. He touched every infant and child, vowing to work to make a better future for them. It took Letivi all of the rest of the day and most of the next day to complete his meetings with every single inhabitant of the village. The villagers were awed by the unprecedented, but much welcomed, effort of Letivi to meet and greet them. They were unceasing in thanking God for sending them such a competent and inspiring chief.

One reason Letivi made an effort to meet everyone in the village was his fear that people did not know him up close and only saw his very light skin. Letivi wanted the villagers to know he was very much one of them in spite of his pale complexion. He was fond of saying, "I may be white to you, but my heart is black and I am of your blood."

The more people got to know Letivi, the more they could look beyond his skin color and see his true character. For them, the character of a person was what counted the most. After only a short time with Letivi, they felt comfortable with him, and they were convinced they could trust him. They were impressed by the way Letivi spoke their language so perfectly and by his ability to weave intelligently proverbs and parables into his speech. His hand and facial gestures were also typical of what was common among them. They felt at home with Letivi and were ready to follow him without hesitation. They could see he was a natural leader and destined to be a great chief. Everyone was immensely proud of having a chief with Letivi's formidable qualities.

While Letivi was making sure his people knew him and felt at ease with him, a handful of senior elders and Kontor were preparing a place for his initiation ceremonies in a remote location in the forest on the top of Mount Ataku near their original village. Only a few knew the secrets involved with the process required to prepare a chief to sit on the royal stool. Those secrets had been passed down over the generations. It was not really known what transpired during the five-day initiation period, but in the past those men selected as chiefs came back from the initiation course profoundly changed. It was known that much of what happened involved the grandfathers and the spirit world, as they would have to bless the new chief before he could rule.

The day arrived when Letivi had to accompany Kontor to the secluded place in the mountaintop forest. He was informed by his grandfather, Chief Gyasi (who was not a part of the indoctrination program), that he would depart early the next morning with the elderly Kontor. Letivi rushed to see his mother to inform her, the trees, and plants he grew up with about the big event. They were so proud of Letivi and could not stop congratulating and encouraging him. It was hard for them to believe that the child they knew so well would be the village chief. Knowing Letivi as well as they did, they could interpret his selection as chief as a very good omen for the future of the village.

Letivi joined Kontor at first light the next morning. Kontor was very old, but spry and he started walking up the mountain path at a lively pace. Along the way Kontor revealed to Letivi, "I knew well your real father, Bobovovi. There are no secrets in the village that I do not know."

Letivi tried to act as if Kontor's words did not surprise him. "Dear wise one, I am happy to know you knew my father. Please tell me about him."

"Your father was a beautiful, but very ignorant young Whiteman from America whose destiny waited for him in our village. From the time he arrived, his presence caused great commotion in the spirit world, causing them to reach out in unprecedented ways to your father. In particular, the moon god and the old baobab worked to bring him to their world. Like you, your father was a moonchild, but he did not know this. Your father was the only person ever known in our history to have ridden a moonbeam and to be swallowed by the baobab, which transformed him into a spirit. As such, your father is here with us as we speak. Your father represents the most important miracle that has ever occurred in our history."

Letivi was greatly moved by Kontor's words. Nobody had ever spoken to him about his father in that way. "Wise one. Please tell me more about my father. I know so little about him. I hope one day he will return to this Earth so I can meet him."

Kontor stopped for a moment and struggled to catch his breath, as they trudged up the steep mountain path before saying, "Your father knew nothing about Africa before arriving in our village. I, and a few others, including your mother's predecessor, Mama Ati-wono, had been instructed by Chief Yofu to teach him the basics about our traditions and customs so that he could do a better job of staying out of trouble. He did cause too much trouble, but he was allowed to stay among us because he was so loved by the spirits and the grandfathers were very attached to him. We were patient with him, as we believed in time his purpose among us would be revealed."

Kontor continued, as the mountain path became steeper and choked by the surrounding bush, "Four other elders and I accompanied your father that night to the old baobab. We were expecting him to come out of the baobab in the morning in possession of the secret of the five leaves, which had been lost to us for generations. We were shocked when he did not come out. He has never been seen since that full moon night. On that day, the opening in the old baobab closed and its branches, which had been barren for years, sprouted leaves and large fruits. We did all we could to urge the old baobab to return him, but the baobab never answered us."

Letivi followed closely every word spoken by Kontor about his father. That was an exceedingly precious moment for Letivi and he relished every word he heard about his father. "Most respected wise one, thank you for telling me so much about my father. I wish to share with you what the old baobab told me when I spent the night of the last full moon next to its trunk. The baobab vibrated slightly when the full moon was directly overhead and said 'soon.' When I heard this word I was convinced that I could not leave the village and I must become chief as quickly as possible. My father is going to return soon and I must be here when he does. I will spend every full moon night with the baobab until my father returns."

After hearing Letivi, Kontor was silent for a few minutes. Looking directly at Letivi he said briefly in his gravelly voice, "I know my son and I agree. You are doing the right thing. I will also be happy to see your father returned to us before I leave this Earth. The days remaining for me are far too few."

Just as Kontor finished those words, the two-hour climb up Mount Ataku's three thousand foot high summit was completed. A senior elder was waiting for them at that point. He led them deep into the thick forest undergrowth, far from any paths, to a small circular clearing that was empty except for a tree in the middle with three top branches sprouting from it. It was called a "tripod" tree and sitting at its top was a clay bowl that had been carefully balanced where the three branches met. Letivi knew the clay bowl contained leaves from a special tree and water that had been blessed by all the top fetish priests of the village. Letivi, Kontor, and the three other senior elders would spend the next five or six days at the foot of that sacred tripod tree.

There was little water and only cassava flour snack food available. Kontor informed Letivi, "You will be eating, drinking, and sleeping very little during our time at this sacred spot. We will ask you to chew and digest a small quantity of bitter leaves from a secret tree. These leaves contain a substance that will put you in a trance for several days. Once in this trance you will be able to see and communicate with the grandfathers and a few spirits. The grandfathers will share with you their secrets and instruct you on how a chief should behave. As chief-to-be, only you can be privy to this information."

Letivi could not say anything to Kontor and the others about all he was hearing already from the old trees around them. He was sure that Kontor knew he understood tree language, but that was something he would keep to himself. The trees were abuzz with all kinds of advice and congratulations for him. As he walked just outside the edge of the clearing to relieve himself, Letivi thanked the trees and asked them to be quiet so he could focus on the requirements of his initiation.

When Letivi returned to the center of the clearing, Kontor raised his voice so all could hear. "We must hurry and start this initiation, as the grandfathers are waiting anxiously to receive Letivi."

Kontor was given a small cloth bag by one of the elders and he withdrew a handful of small leaves. He approached Letivi and said, "My son, please do not be afraid. Stay strong and be full of courage. I know you will do well. We will be at your side until you return to us. Please greet the grandfathers for us. We envy this great opportunity being afforded to you. You leave us as a young man; you will return to us as a mature adult who is our chief. This is your destiny and the destiny of our village!"

Kontor handed the leaves to Letivi, saying, "Chew well these leaves and swallow them and their juice. You best sit down and prepare yourself to travel to the other world."

Letivi did as instructed. A few minutes after he had finished swallowing the last of the leaves, he went into convulsions. Foaming from the mouth, he fell backward on the ground. His body shook as if he were having a seizure. After about ten minutes, he lay on the ground perfectly still on his back with his hazel-green eyes wide open and his pupils fully dilated. He was not asleep, but he was not awake either. He was in the other world. Kontor and the others sat down around him, prepared to take turns observing him around-the-clock until he returned to Earth. They would be watching for any signs that would require action on their part.

For Letivi, it was as if he had died and gone to a celestial place where there were many dreamlike figures representing the grandfathers sitting around him and, from time-to-time, ghostlike spirits flying through the air in rapid flight, making inscrutable moaning sounds. As Letivi adjusted to his transported state, things became a bit clearer and he remembered to be on the lookout for his father's spirit. The grandfathers told him many things, passing on the knowledge of generations and revealing secrets only chiefs could know. They welcomed him among them and said they recognized him as a very special chief.

The grandfathers were happy he was a moonchild. There had not been a moonchild as a chief since their very first chief hundreds of years ago. They said he was replacing that first chief, and therefore, he had to be given the same markings that chief had. Those with him on Earth had to give him those markings before he returned to them. They drew an outline of Letivi's body on the ground with a stick and indicated where scarification had to be done on his body. Two cuts in the shape of a half-moon would be made, one on the top of each cheek. A heavier half-moon scar would be cut in the middle of his chest. Small outlines of a full moon would be cut on each shoulder.

The grandfathers told Letivi to rise up and draw the same images on the ground so those with him on Earth could begin making those markings on his body. He could not return to Earth until those permanent scars were administered to his body. Letivi forced himself to do as instructed. As soon as he moved, Kontor and the others jumped to their feet to see what Letivi would do. When Letivi picked up a stick and drew on the ground the body scars he needed, they pulled from another bag the special iron scarification knives they had brought with them for that expected ritual.

Letivi also indicated with his fingers where his scars should be cut and how they should be shaped. The elders immediately recognized that the requested scars were the moonchild scars they had heard about in their oral history. They knew those were the scars of their first chief. They were very excited about doing rare moonchild scars. They began the bloody work of cutting into Letivi's tender flesh in the prescribed manner at the places indicated.

As Letivi lay flat on the ground, one elder who specialized in scarification delicately cut the half-moon shape under his eyes, high up on top of his cheekbones. He then used a thicker blade to cut the full moon shape on each shoulder. With an even thicker blade, a heavier half-moon cut was made in the middle of Letivi's upper chest. The blood that flowed profusely was mopped up with the leaves of a medicinal bush. Those leaves helped stop the flow of flood and contained a substance that was an effective disinfectant. In less than an hour, the scarification of Letivi ordered by the grandfathers was completed. Letivi's drug-induced trance prevented him from feeling anything.

The grandfathers continued their constant barrage of information that Letivi had to retain as a chief. He learned about all the chiefs and their accomplishments. They repeated the oral history of the village from the time it was founded on the mountain nearly four hundred years ago. They gave examples of how a chief should behave and speak. The grandfathers told him how to contact them when he needed their advice. When the grandfathers stopped talking, Letivi asked them for permission to speak. "Thank you, my grandfathers. I am honored to be among you. I am immensely appreciative of all that you have told me and I promise to follow always your guidance. I have only one question: Where is my father, Bobovovi?"

Several grandfathers responded in unison. "Your father is no longer in our world, as he has headed back to your world. You should see him soon. Watch the skies for a sign of his coming."

Letivi continued to lay prostrate on the ground with his eyes wide open for two more days. Kontor and the elders watched over him night and day, lighting a small kerosene lantern at night. They drank little and ate only a few handfuls of cassava flour. They continued to wipe the wounds made by Letivi's scarification ceremony with medicinal leaves. On the morning of the fifth day, they saw Letivi close his eyes. They knew it was a sign that he was almost ready to return to them. It took several hours more for Letivi to begin to stir. One elder left the group to return to the village to ask the women in the chief's compound to bring food, water, and clothes for their new chief, and to instruct the village criers to inform the people to prepare to receive their new chief that afternoon. The long awaited news ignited much excitement and rejoicing in the village.

Letivi was slow to regain consciousness. For him, it was as if he had passed out for a few hours instead of five days. He was helped to sit up and given some water to sip. Letivi sat motionless, as he looked slowly around and at the places on his body that had been cut. He felt nauseated and was experiencing some pain from where his body had been scarred. It took him an hour to get his bearings. He asked to speak alone with Kontor. He had trouble with his speech, but he was able to say haltingly to Kontor, "The grandfathers told me my father has already left to return to Earth. We will see him soon."

Kontor quickly retorted, "That is good news, but please know that what the grandfathers told you was for your ears only. You need not tell me or anyone else anymore."

They walked slowly through the forest to where the path to the village began. The elders held wobbly Letivi at his sides to help him walk. Letivi was in a stupor, weak, and still very much disoriented. They waited at the spot for the women to come with food, water, and chief clothes for Letivi. The women arrived in short order. They bowed their heads in respect for their new chief, deposited the buckets and baskets they had brought, and quickly departed without looking directly at Letivi. Nobody was supposed to see the chief until he was presented to the village as a whole.

Kontor and the elders gave Letivi ample time to eat and drink, and set a bucket full of water and bar of soap behind a nearby tree so he could bathe. After Letivi ate and drank as much as he could, he took a bath, and then he was dressed in the royal chief clothes. He was also given the chief's royal staff to carry and the chief's ornamental cap was placed carefully on his head. When he was fully dressed, Kontor and the other elders stepped back and hailed their new chief. Kontor happily proclaimed, "Chief Letivi, your people await you. We are ready to escort you down the mountain when you are ready to go."

Letivi raised his chief's staff in the air with his right hand and in a weak voice said, "I thank all of you for your service to me and our village. I hope I can continue to count upon your unfailing support. I believe I have recovered and I am now sufficiently strong enough to return to the village. Let us begin the first leg of a journey to a brighter future for our beloved village."

CHAPTER TWENTY-ONE
GEMINI'S GHOST

The years had not been kind to Gemini. Shortly after J.B.'s disappearance, the big oil refinery in Gemini closed. The refinery was the main source of income for most of its inhabitants. The people of Gemini were very upset when its New York owners decided abruptly to shut it down. That massive loss of livelihoods obliged most people to move out of town to search for work elsewhere. Within a few years, Gemini almost became a ghost town. Its schools, hospital, and most of its stores closed. The only people remaining were the very elderly, the lazy, and the unemployable. All town maintenance and basic services ceased to operate. The streets filled up with discarded trash and wayward tumbleweeds. Gemini had truly become one of many old towns in Kansas that were a mere shadow of their former prominence.

The park dedicated to J.B. fell into disuse; it was no longer recognizable as a public park and place of adoration. There were few people remaining in town who could remember J.B. and why there was a park where he once lived. Only a few years back, a colorful annual festival was held in the park on the anniversary of J.B.'s disappearance to celebrate him. One of the events of that special day was for everyone to walk along J.B.'s path. Many vendors came to the festival to sell vintage J.B. T-shirts, descendants of his goldfish and cats, and assorted memorabilia that honored J.B.'s memory. Some participants in the festival dressed up in J.B. costumes and acted like the ghosts of J.B. Many believed J.B.'s ghost was among them and referred to J.B. as "Gemini's Ghost." That enjoyable festival dwindled to an end as the town headed toward near extinction.

All traces of J.B. were erased by the passage of time and hard circumstances imposed on Gemini. The once revered local folk hero and widely known legend had been forgotten. His unusual disappearance and the legacy he left behind were only noticed by the very curious who delved deeply into state libraries and newspaper records. Nobody cared anymore about J.B. or what he had meant to Gemini for so many years. J.B.'s celebrity status had become only a footnote in the history of a town whose record was already filed away in dusty and lonely archives.

None of that mattered to J.B. In his bizarre manner, the entire time he resided in Gemini was totally focused on returning to Ataku. In his inner being he knew the only way to do that was to worship unceasingly the old baobab, pleading with it to accept his return and to work with the moon to agree to transport him back to Ataku. He knew innately that the only way he could return to Ataku was to ride a moonbeam, and such a ride could only occur if the baobab accepted it. His irrepressible desire to return to Ataku could only happen if the moon and the baobab committed for the first time to work together to help a human travel through time and space across the globe.

Nobody in Gemini could have imagined the bright flash some people many observed on that full moon night was related to the mysterious disappearance of J.B. Later, some people remarked that Gemini began to fall on hard times soon after J.B. disappeared. People began to speculate that there was some kind of obscure connection between J.B. and the demise of their town. One old lady remarked, "J.B. was our good luck charm and now we are out of luck."

The eccentric J.B. had achieved what he had been seeking for almost twenty years each time the moon was full. Just as it had done many years ago in Ataku, the moon sent a beam down to take J.B. away on his journey back to Ataku. A moonbeam snatched J.B. and whisked him away in a twinkling of an eye. The moon did not take him straight to Ataku, but parked him in the spirit world until the old baobab said it was ready to receive him. Years were like days in that world so it is hard to say how long J.B. was kept in suspended animation in the other world. During that time, J.B. lay in a coma, not knowing what had happened to him or where he was.

The grandfathers and spirits excitedly observed the human sleeping among them and knew his case was pending until the old and stubborn baobab made his mind up about when would be the best time for J.B. to return to him. They knew J.B. when he lived briefly among them as the young Bobovovi and they were impressed that somehow he had managed to return. They were also intrigued about how old and ugly he looked. One grandfather commented, "It is too bad he did not stay with us because he would not have aged."

J.B. remained in limbo for a long time in the other world. It is known that his body quivered for an instant when Letivi made clear contact with the old baobab. The grandfathers and spirits surmised that in J.B.'s mind he was seeing what was happening on Earth between his son Letivi and the baobab. J.B. also heard the old baobab say, "Soon," and that utterance by the old tree sent a quiver of anticipation through his body like a low-voltage bolt of electricity. That quivering also alerted all those in the other world that J.B.'s layover among them would soon end.

The grandfathers and spirits kept a close watch on J.B.'s condition. If need be, they were ready to lend a hand with his onward voyage. They knew J.B. was earthbound, as the old baobab had agreed to his return and was negotiating with the moon his ride back to Ataku. J.B.'s complexion seemed to brighten and sometimes his fingers and toes wiggled. A small smile appeared on his face. One grandfather commented, "J.B.'s new found happiness is almost making him come alive. He must be anticipating in his mind good things ahead."

J.B. was not the only one anticipating happiness. His son, Chief Letivi, was about to be received by the people of Ataku as their chief for the first time. As Letivi began to descend from the mountain to be received by his people, he kept one eye on the path in front of him and one eye on the sky for the sign the grandfathers told him about while he was in a trance. He knew something would happen in the sky. When it did, he had to go immediately to the old baobab and look for his father. Letivi was overwhelmed by all he planned to do as chief and the prospect of meeting his father for the first time. All his hopes were pinned on good things happening when the next full moon would occur in a few weeks. There was no doubt in Letivi's mind that better times lay ahead.

CHAPTER TWENTY-TWO
BAOBAB BLESSING

Letivi gazed down the mountainside to where throngs of people in the village had filled the passageways to await his arrival. There were dancing and drumming groups among them. People were singing, dancing, and shouting loud praises to the gods and grandfathers for placing Letivi on the royal stool. It was a joyous, noisy event and everyone was waiting to see their new chief and hear his inaugural speech.

Kontor and the elders who had been with him on the mountain led the way through the crowds, asking people to make way for their new chief. Letivi remained silent and kept a stone face, as he had been told to do during his initiation ceremonies. People were taken aback by Letivi's aged appearance and his new scars were very noticeable. The aura projected by Letivi's chiefly demeanor deeply impressed the people who bowed their heads in respect as Letivi walked by.

When they arrived in front of Chief Yofu's compound, Letivi was told to stand on an elevated wooden platform in front of what would now be his house. Letivi slowly climbed the half-dozen steps up to the top of the small platform, taking care not to trip on the very ample and colorful chief's gown he was wearing. Once at the top, he stood straight and looked around in a steely and very stately manner. He tried to look into the eyes of all who had gathered for the important event.

He stood still for several minutes, and just after taking a look at the distant sky, he raised in his right hand the chief's royal cane. That gesture brought silence to the crowd. In a booming and very different, more authoritative voice than he previously possessed, he called at the top of his voice, "My people! My People! My People! Beginning today your new chief is here to serve you the best he can for all his life. My main goal is to make Ataku the most happy and prosperous village in the country. The best way to do this is to ensure all men and women have gainful employment and are committed to the best interests of the village. The key to achieving this goal is an appropriate education for everyone and changing any practices that impede our progress."

Chief Letivi concluded by saying, "We must all work together in harmony to preserve peace and create conditions favorable to our advancement. We must dedicate ourselves to passing on a better world to those who follow us. I know I can count on your full collaboration. Thank you for your gracious reception today and all that you have already done to achieve progress in our village. I plan to meet immediately with our elders and clan leaders to begin discussing a road map for accelerating the development of our village. May the gods and the grandfathers always look over you."

Letivi turned and entered his chief's compound and headed for the big circular meeting hangar. He stopped briefly in the compound to address the family members of Chief Yofu. "I am pleased to see all of you. I ask that you continue as you did during the time of Chief Yofu. I hope I can count on your continued support. I look forward to living here with you."

The women and children in the compound happily responded in unison, "We salute you, our chief, and we promise our entire devotion to you and your mission."

Chief Gyasi followed Letivi closely, whispering to him, "I am very proud of you, my grandson, and I, too, commit my full support to you and your chiefly mission."

When all were seated, Letivi rose and proceeded to shake the hand of every elder and clan chief, thanking them for coming to the meeting on such short notice and for all their support. As he shook hands, he looked straight into the eyes of each man. That sort of direct eye contact with a chief was a first for those village leaders. They all felt captivated by Letivi's aura and the way he had taken charge of the village from the onset of his chieftaincy.

Letivi quickly opened the meeting in a businesslike fashion. He started by saying, "First, I want to thank Chief Gyasi for all his hard work as a regent. He will always be my chief and I count on him to serve me as my senior advisor. Please, let us all applaud Chief Gyasi."

After a brief, but enthusiastic applause, Letivi continued, "You heard what I told the people. This meeting is about agreeing on the key milestones of our village development plan. In this plan I must insist that education is the key because it opens doors to increasing our participation in the marketplace. This is the only way we can reduce poverty, achieve greater prosperity, and keep up with the rest of the world, which is moving quickly ahead."

The elders and clan chiefs were puzzled by Letivi's words and did not know what to say. One senior elder rose and said, "Our dear chief. What you say sounds very interesting, but we do not understand. Can you please give an example of what you mean?"

Letivi smiled and responded in a kind and respectful manner. "If we do not have anything to sell in the marketplace, we will always remain poor. Every healthy person must be enabled to sell goods or their labor in the marketplace in order to increase their incomes, and thus, reduce their poverty. A truly poor person is one who does not interact with the marketplace. It is our job to find a way for every person to sell something in the most profitable local, national, regional, or international marketplaces. A key element to achieving these objectives will be resolving our energy constraints. We must manage our village like a well-run private company."

When Letivi finished speaking, there was a long pause as everyone looked at each other with raised eyebrows, indicating confusion over what their new chief was saying. Chief Gyasi interrupted the silence. "Chief Letivi, there is still some confusion in our minds. Maybe the best way to proceed is to take your bold, but very attractive plan for our village a step at a time. What are the next steps?"

Letivi spoke more affirmatively. "I understand your uneasiness, but we have no time to lose. If we are to get ahead, we must run very fast to stay in the same place. In the days ahead, we must elaborate a detailed business plan that inventories all we have and all we want, and lays out a road map of how we get from where we are to where we want to go. But, even before this plan is completed, there are obvious things that we need to do as quickly as possible."

After a brief pause to let Chief Letivi's words sink deeply into the minds of all present, Chief Gyasi again said, "Very well. Let us designate a working committee to devise our village development plan; but, in the meantime, please name for us those actions we should take now."

Letivi could not wait to say. "I am ready to begin working tomorrow morning with a small group of you, or those you designate to represent you, on a draft of our development plan. For now, I ask that each clan chief identify the brightest children in the village. I would like to have a list of these children, their ages and sex, their level of schooling, and their school performance records. This list should contain an equal number of boys and girls. We must make sure the best and brightest of our children will receive a good education and become eligible for attractive employment opportunities locally or abroad. We must work so that all our children grow up well and find jobs. This means not having more children than we can assure good futures."

Letivi's words had the men's minds reeling, causing them to become short of breath. Letivi continued speaking. "I know this is too much for you to digest on my first day as your chief, but I assure you that I have thought about this for years, and what I say is the best way ahead for us. We must identify what the marketplace needs today and tomorrow in terms of goods, labor, and services so that we can position ourselves over time to respond and profit from the opportunities offered by the marketplace. It is a very competitive world and we must learn to compete with the best of them!"

Chief Gyasi stood up and addressed everyone. "Let us thank our chief for these brilliant ideas. We need to discuss his ideas with our respective families and come back to Chief Letivi tomorrow with the information he asks. A team can also begin preparing our development plan tomorrow."

Following those words, all stood and applauded Chief Letivi. Each man present said at once, "We agree and commit ourselves and all our followers to your inspiring and illuminating leadership."

Letivi thanked the men and bid them farewell and safe return to their respective family compounds. Letivi informed them, "I am always available to you. The only time I will be out of touch is on full moon nights." The men understood without hesitation that a moonchild must be with the moon goddess when the moon was full.

As each man filed out of the meeting room, Letivi shook his hands with a loud and satisfactory finger snap and patted each man on the shoulder, thanking each man again for their support and telling each firmly, "Together we shall overcome and advance."

Letivi escorted the men out of his new compound, and as he did, he gazed at the sky for any special signs. He knew that the full moon was only a few days off, and thus, he was constantly watching the sky for any signs that might indicate when the moon and old baobab had conspired to bring back his father.

In the days that followed the initial meeting of village leaders there were many more meetings. Chief Letivi and a small team worked around-the-clock to collect the information needed to design the village development plan. There were many discussions and sometimes heated debates occurred. Letivi encouraged the participation of everyone and insisted on the involvement of women leaders. He would often say that the village could not advance if its women did not also advance.

The village was energized like never before and all the people were galvanized into action behind the enlightened leadership of their very honest and competent chief, whose only interest was improving the lot of his people. The level of enthusiasm was at an unbelievable high level. People began to believe that by working together they could achieve anything. Minds were opened to new possibilities. Hopes for a better and more fulfilling future were mushrooming. People became passionate about making a better future for themselves and their descendants. Those were exciting and inspiring times for the people of Ataku.

As each group completed a meeting with Chief Letivi during those busy times of rolling out courses of actions to bring more prosperity to the village, Letivi would kindly escort them in a very cordial and respectful manner out of his compound. When each group had departed, he would go to the adjoining grandfathers' compound and leave an offering for them while he pleaded for their support and guidance. While in the compound he would search the sky in all directions for a sign.

The day of the monthly full moon arrived and Letivi could feel his heart beat faster and his body temperature rise. He made everyone aware that on that day he had to remain alone. All day long his eyes were scanning the sky for any sign that would tell him the time had come for him to wait at the old baobab for the return of his father. In any event, Letivi was preparing to camp out next to the baobab on that full moon night.

Just before the night fell and Letivi was about ready to stealthily head for his rendezvous with the old baobab, he looked up to see a sight he had never seen before. The unusually bright full moon was rising over the distant treetops and arching just below it for an instant was a pulsating rainbow. There was no doubt in Letivi's mind that it was the sign indicating his father would be returned that night.

Letivi rushed along back paths to where the old baobab reigned. He went straight to the baobab, laid his hands on its bulbous trunk, and prayed out loud in tree language, "Most respected one. I saw the sign in the sky and came as fast as I could. Thank you for working with the moon to return my father. I will always honor you. I wait now for the miracle to happen."

The full moon was moving slowly up and across the center of the dark sky, casting an almost blinding swath of bright white light as it climbed to its zenith. Letivi knew that the most likely time his father would be sent back was when the moon was directly over the baobab. He stripped off his clothes so he could fully bathe in the light of the moon and ensure there was not any barrier between him and the moon. He called loudly at the moon to let it know he was present and waiting. He danced around the baobab tree like a madman, howling like a wolf at the moon to the extent his voice would allow. It was as if the moon had taken control of its child and was demonstrating it was in command of the moonlit night.

Almost unnoticed was a dot of bluish light that streaked rapidly across the sky like a meteorite fragment being pulled unwillingly by gravity down to an alien Earth. Letivi stopped in his tracks, not because of the meteorite flash, but because the moon, which was directly overhead, transfixed him with moon rays, penetrating every pore of his sweaty body. For a moment Letivi was not on Earth, he was in some kind of eerie never-never land. Letivi's trance-like condition ended abruptly when he heard a soft thud of something landing nearby on the ground.

Letivi regained consciousness and turned to see a mist-like white dust rising from the ground near him. The mist quickly evaporated and Letivi could see a human figure lying on the ground. He ran the few yards to the figure and knelt down beside the form of an old, baldheaded Whiteman dressed only in a white jersey and faded red boxer shorts. The knowledge that it was his father, Bobovovi, penetrated deeply into his being, making him dizzy and faint. He struggled to keep his strength and his composure as he stared at every inch of the odd-looking Whiteman who lay flat on his back on the ground before him.

Bobovovi began to show signs of life. Letivi grasped his hand and with tears in his eyes and much emotion managed to say, "Father, your son is here. Welcome back. You are home."

Upon hearing Letivi's sincere words, Bobovovi opened his greenish eyes and smiled as he looked at his son's face. Letivi could see his father was suffering. He placed his face next to his and embraced him tightly. With Letivi's ears very near his father's mouth, Bobovovi struggled mightily to mutter a few words. "My son, I am happy to be where I belong. I love you. Tell your mother I always loved her. I wish I could stay, but I am at my end."

With his last word, Bobovovi's eyes closed and his skimpily clad body became very still. Letivi remained the rest of the night next to his father with his arms wrapped around him. When the sun rose, there was another unlikely, but vivid rainbow in the distant sky. Letivi knew that was the moon's way of saying good-bye and confirming she had kept her promise by returning his father.

The baobab presented an even more startling sight. Its barren branches had born many leaves and fruits. Hundreds of little white birds chirping an enchanting melody in unison covered it. He stood up to look at his father's body, which had been quickly covered by dozens of rare red-crested chameleons. It was clear to Letivi that it was the old baobab's way of welcoming the return of Bobovovi. His father looked so peaceful in death. An angelic smile remained on his chubby face.

As Letivi turned to thank the old baobab, he readily noticed the old tree's trunk had split wide open and he could see a large empty space inside the tree. He knew he had to carry his father's remains and place them inside the tree. He had no trouble lifting his father's frail body and carrying it the few yards to the grotto within the tree. He carefully laid his father's body on the ground and covered it with an African cloth he had brought with him. He said good-bye to his father for the last time and stepped outside the tree's opening.

As soon as he was outside the tree, Letivi placed his hands on the baobab's roughly gnarled trunk. He spoke again in tree language. "Old and wise one. Thank you for what you have done. My father is at peace now and with you forever. Please take good care of him. I will visit you every full-moon night."

Letivi turned to pick up his clothes and dress himself before going to see his mother to tell her what had happened. He picked up the small bag he had brought and turned to look at the tree one more time. The birds were singing more loudly than ever and had been joined by countless chameleons vigorously swaying their heads back and forth in time with the birds' sweet melody. Letivi was surprised to see that there was no longer an opening in the tree. Somehow the old baobab had silently closed itself around his father's final resting place.

Letivi bid farewell to the baobab and began his walk to his mother's forest enclave on the slope of Mount Ataku. He turned one more time to view the old baobab in all its breathtaking glory. At that moment, he noticed the white marble plaque that had been erected at the base of the baobab's trunk to note Bobovovi's strange disappearance long ago. The sight of the marker caused something to come over Letivi that prompted him to pull the plaque up and take it with him.

For Letivi, the time had come to end Bobovovi's story and put his secret away forever. It was the only way for Bobovovi to enjoy the peace he fully deserved. Bobovovi's time was over. It was now the time for a new generation to have its own miracles and write its own story. Time always marches ahead and time is only kind to those who march with it.

www.ingramcontent.com/pod-product-compliance
Lightning Source LLC
Chambersburg PA
CBHW070614130626
46556CB00001B/361